PRAISE FOR *The Ancestry of Objects*

"Ryckman writes with cool, tightly packed precision on the futile ways people try to fill the emptiness and absence of life with objects and religion and desperate acts . . . A hypnotizing, bleak account of the ways people trap themselves in their own minds."

—*Kirkus Reviews*

"Ryckman's *The Ancestry of Objects* accomplishes a difficult and compelling tension with lyrical prose that ropes readers into a nuanced depiction of the pleasure and pain of human relationships. She renders the figures of her fragmented novel with a stark tenderness, reflecting the beauty and unattractiveness of desire. There are no villains, no heroes, just complications between people whose flaws will draw readers to recognize themselves and our shared yearning to be known."

—Donald Quist, author of *Harbors* and *For Other Ghosts*

"I've always loved Ryckman's fiction, but nothing in the idiosyncratic originality of her short stories prepared me for her stunning novel with its dark eroticism, its plunge into depths of loneliness, and its quest for paradoxical liberation. Her extraordinary narrator lives in a state of erasure but thinks as plural: the social self for whom everything is always "fine"; the guilty, sinful self as defined by the now-dead grandparents; the self who needs to be seen through the outside eye of the absent lover, the absent God; and most of all, the self who feels dead in daily life and alive when courting an exuberant annihilation. In reading this powerful and disturbing short novel, I found myself splitting as well, into the reader who could not put these pages down, and the reader who had to, in order to regain her equilibrium and catch her throttled breath."

—Diane Lefer, award-winning author

playwright, and activist

PRAISE FOR *I Don't Think of You (Until I Do)*

"(Ryckman) has joined the likes of Clarice Lispector, Claudia Rankine, and John Berger."

—Matthew Dickman, author of *Mayakovsky's Revolver*

"Ryckman's reflective novella unfolds in 100 tiny, often forlorn chapters, each micro-numbered (from 0.1 to 10.0) and given a page of its own. Through this, form and content merge, as the narrator attempts to absorb the lessons of a failed long-distance relationship and, in turn, understand herself . . . The isolation of each individual entry underscores this haunting story from beginning to end."

—*Publishers Weekly*

"Keenly felt and fiercely written. Tatiana Ryckman is a revelation."

—Jennifer duBois, author of *Cartwheel*

"Ryckman has written the anti-love story within all of us. A book so earnest and sharp in its examination of heartbreak, it will make you ache for all the people you haven't even loved yet."

—T Kira Madden,
author of *Long Live the Tribe of Fatherless Girls*

"Tatiana Ryckman has written a wonder; a remarkably accomplished work of such keen observation and emotional complexity as to rival those texts—Maggie Nelson's *Bluets* come to mind—with which it shares some literary DNA. Ryckman is a ruthless investigator of reckless desire . . . *I Don't Think of You (Until I Do)* asks—newly, stunningly, with precise prose chiseled from stone—what it is we're meant to do when the source of our appetite is beyond the realm of our own cognition, and following this narrator in pursuit of the unanswerable is a reading experience as gutting as it is thrilling. One finishes this book with the simple thought: Now here is a person."

—Vincent Scarpa

THE ANCESTRY OF OBJECTS

Tatiana Ryckman

DEEP VELLUM PUBLISHING
DALLAS, TEXAS

Deep Vellum Publishing
3000 Commerce St., Dallas, Texas 75226
deepvellum.org · @deepvellum

Deep Vellum is a 501c3 nonprofit literary arts organization
founded in 2013 with the mission to bring
the world into conversation through literature.

Support for this publication has been provided in part by grants from the National Endowment for the Arts, the Texas Commission on the Arts, the City of Dallas Office of Arts and Culture's ArtsActivate program, and the Moody Fund for the Arts:

ISBNs: 978-1-64605-025-3 (paperback) | 978-1-64605-026-0 (ebook)

LIBRARY OF CONGRESS CATALOGING IN PUBLICATION DATA

Names: Ryckman, Tatiana, author.
Title: The ancestry of objects / Tatiana Ryckman.
Description: First edition. | Dallas, Texas : Deep Vellum Publishing, 2020.
Identifiers: LCCN 2020010104 (print) | LCCN 2020010105 (ebook) | ISBN 9781646050253 (paperback) | ISBN 9781646050260 (ebook)
Subjects: LCSH: Psychological fiction.
Classification: LCC PS3618.Y353 A69 2020 (print) | LCC PS3618.Y353 (ebook) | DDC 813/.6—dc23
LC record available at https://lccn.loc.gov/2020010104
LC ebook record available at https://lccn.loc.gov/2020010105

Cover Artwork and Design © 2019 Sonnenzimmer

Interior Layout and Typesetting by Kirby Gann

Text set in Bembo, a typeface modeled on typefaces cut by Francesco Griffo for Aldo Manuzio's printing of *De Aetna* in 1495 in Venice.

PRINTED IN THE UNITED STATES OF AMERICA

ACKNOWLEDGMENTS

I am forever indebted to Yaddo for the time and space to write, and to the many readers whose guidance and encouragement made this work possible: Boomer Pinches, T Kira Madden, Ian Patrick Miller, Lisa Wells, Charlie Clements, Rob Reynolds, Levis Keltner, Caitlyn Renee Miller, Jen Maidenberg, and Emily Roberts. I am grateful to Nick and Nadine of Sonnenzimmer for their amazing work on the cover, and to my publisher, Will Evans, whose patience and insistence brought this manuscript to life. Finally, I could never have written this book without Ed and Jennie and the house that they built.

The premeditation of death is the premeditation of liberty;
he who has learned to die has unlearned to serve.

—Michel de Montaigne

PROLOGUE

When he pushes us over the kitchen sink and lifts our dress, we watch the fading sun glint off the faucet. On the first strike, waves move through our skin and he pulls his hand back; we hear the hollow crack before we feel the sting. We anticipate the second slap and brace ourself with whitening knuckles. A ceramic finch watches, detached. The edge of the sink is smooth but unforgiving where it digs into our ribs just below our breasts. We think Tits; we command him to Feel my tits, but we don't know where the words come from or go.

The first waterfall of moisture runs down our thigh with the sweat. It splits into two streams at the knee. His fingers wear the memory of her hair, and the sweat of our lower back mixes with the salt of her tears and the salt of his come landing like a flock of birds on our back. He smooths the cream over our spine like icing. He licks and puts his hand to our mouth to taste.

The glaze of his fingers fills the air in front of our face with the scent of warm dough.

Her tears and hair and our sweat and his come scrape onto our teeth, and we taste the hollow sound of each slap echoing through the porn of our memory. He relaxes his hand in our mouth until we let go. His lips touch down on our back in the erratic pattern of ejaculate. He rubs the come in like lotion and it dries into a tight flaky skin that peels like a sunburn.

He walks through the space he's claimed and sits. The chair rolls a few inches just as it used to every time our grandmother fell into it and slid across the kitchen tile before bumping into the table, shuffling papers and silverware into stacks.

As we move toward him we don't think about what we've done; we think instead about this man: the clean crease pressed into his pants, the good shape he's in, considering, about how easily he manufactures a smile, a history, money. Our own history has been reduced to the last few moments of our mutual existence, of his silent panic, and the wife's starved fingers as they wander the sparse forest of his straight chest hair. We think the phrase Snake in the grass. Think Babes in the Wood. Think Hansel and Gretel and their trail of bread. Think of the trails left by the wife's tears when the man says first I love you, and then, But—

When we imagine him leaving her, he is already mistaking her hair for ours and does not notice the black makeup on his lips when he kisses her closed eyes goodbye.

When the man wipes her tears away, his fingers claim he is sensitive. And she whispers But—

and then,

I love you.

And they do not hear the things they are not saying.

His long fingers will work around the familiar shape of her, and she will think this means he is changing his mind. That he'll stay. And when, for a moment, it seems he might cry, she'll believe he is repenting.

But he will be saying goodbye.

We lean against the counter and leak onto the linoleum floor. We think of the stain he's made in the house, in us, and wait for the moment when he will leave and we can toy with the lonely wetness of our cunt and the house, the whole house holding us in a warm echo. We will come fondling the bruises he's left.

THE ANCESTRY OF OBJECTS

We learn the man:

When he comes in with a bag, he wants to stay the night. When he cooks at our stove, we pour another glass of wine. We rub the dry fabric of his shirtback lightly until the prints burn off our fingertips. We grip loosely the knob of his elbow and he tells us the history of the day. A good day. Twenty dollars in an old coat pocket, a client pleased, a baffling sum of money that is easier understood as an example of how little we know—about his day, about his fingers when they are not wrapping themselves around our throat, about the desert that lies between us—than of his own work done well.

He finishes his story with a smile and: It was good—Now it's good. He moves his mouth to ours and sets down the old spatula, plastic handle disfigured with heat. He slides his hand from our hip to the soft flesh of our ass and pulls us to him. He says he can be very generous and we resent instantly the implication that we have been bought. That we are indentured. That anything that is ours to give is owed or perhaps already owned by the man. He radiates a salesman's thin integrity. We enjoy the tottering infant of hate we've conceived for him and cultivate it, so we laugh, we pretend that he's said nothing. We take his hand and examine the roadmap of his palm. We joke: This long one must be money, maybe the shorter one is life.

We are thankful for the distraction of water boiling over, spilling white foam across the oven top.

And the first time:

We meet the man at the expensive bar while privately celebrating the end of our life.

The toaster we will throw in the bath.

The car that might run too long in the garage.

The many pills that remain from those who have gone before us.

After "we" and "regret" and "to inform you," the words mean nothing: Streamline, technological advancement, efficiency. We are replaceable, so we will be replaced. Our life, so long unnoticed even by us, suddenly accelerating toward an inevitable end. We can come in, the letter says, to pick up our final paycheck. Otherwise, it will be mailed.

To be free of the daily commute, of the way people arrange themselves at lunch at a distance from us, of the news overheard rather than delivered—to be free of these unencounters would be a solution to the problem of our limited existence if there were something to take its place. The way the other women whispered their secret futures in anticipation of this end: A father who needs to be cared for. A sister who's been asking her to move closer to home. A job that's already been interviewed for.

But we've learned already that our freedom is a more difficult cage to escape than oppression.

On the first day after we receive the letter, after pressing the crescent shape of our nails into the soft skin of our biceps, we model the fantasies of the end of our job and house/home on the end of times our grandparents warned of in lectures we did not listen to. They begin with the appearance of The Beast and then the flight to the caves, and finally, for us, the third or fourth or millionth advent of nothing. A holy final void.

The new meaninglessness of days makes the hours roll out like cruel waves, languid and unconcerned. We are panicked by the disappearance of obligations that had for so long sufficed for purpose. And beyond the duress, admonishment for it. What right do we have to our inconsolableness? The house is inherited, paid for. We could live for a few months, if we could live under the unbearable crush of time. We are not destitute, just precarious. Concerned not with how to lift ourself from the bottom of this pit, but how much farther still is the fall? What sort of future exists for someone who has become obsolete?

We mourn too the end of endless days filled with the delicate dictation of biological errors. We miss in advance the responsibility to witness the repeated failure of body after body described by the doctor; we meditate on the comforting weight of everyone's fragile lives as narrated through headphones, the familiar cadence of a woman's voice reading without emotion the tumors and fractures lit up from behind *comma* from within—the voice of quick and unremarkably slow deaths and injuries of strangers so ingrained in our mind that they seem to foretell our own slow death *period* Her calm voice the one we use to describe our frustrations with traffic in the street outside the window, the voice that narrates the news of the day. The woman's voice, the invisible doctor's voice, recites the brokenness of strangers as we digest our breakfast. It is the voice we use when we defend ourself against the drawl of ancient, well-meaning reproaches. Our grandparents' easy unkindness composing the endless loop of our childhood mistake. The mistake of existing. And in the bathroom mirror, the emotionless voice of dictation is ours when we unscold ourself: We are notbad. We are notsinful.

Now, now, we say with bitterness for our training in self-flagellation. We wish again that they would die but remember, again, there's no need. Everyone is already dead. Except for us.

At the bar the woman's voice dictates the book we are reading in the poor illumination of mood lighting: *And as I walked on* comma *I was lonely no longer* period

When he sits at the bar, waiting for his table and his woman, we see from the corner of our eye that he will speak to us, and when he asks what we are reading we resent him for kicking the crutch of loneliness out from under us like the job, gone, and one day the house, gone, and soon, life, gone. Us, gone.

He has taken her out for dinner, and while she is in the bathroom he takes our time because he does not know it is ours. Because he is generous and believes his attention is a gift. Because perhaps he is afraid of moments alone. And he asks about the book as if we brought ourself for him. We lift it so he can read the title without our needing to speak. We imagine him mouthing the words, reading them like an analog clock. We don't need evidence to water the seed of our malice.

We attempt to carry on despite the intrusion but

manage only to reread *Now* comma *don't think my opinion on these matters is final* comma *he seemed to say* comma *just because I'm stronger and more of a man than you are* period

First time? he asks and we shake our head no. As she crosses the floor of the restaurant on her return from the restroom he adds with unanticipated compassion: It's funny, but I never expect him to die.

We look past the yellowed pages and see the delicate lines by his eyes make an estuary of sadness. His lips tighten into a resigned smile, subtle but controlled, and we believe in that moment that he could have cracked easily like the thin bones in her wrists.

Me too, we think, maybe say aloud, without thinking, to the nothing that is listening. His face is a mask of politeness. We nod to acknowledge her, but she doesn't see us, doesn't need to see us because he is generous. She is wearing a new dress. They are shown to a table and float away on a cloud made of a life empty of complication. When we try to pay for our drinks, the tab has been taken care of, and we are ashamed. We are caught between needing generosity and dying in it. Between wading into the terrifying void that lies ahead and enjoying the excruciating final moments.

We think of the momentary unveiling of the man's sadness.

And of the celebratory red of our own blood merging with water.

At night the house holds us like the thin shell around a yolk. We slide out of our shoes at the door. A small, dark enclosure crowded with sweaters and rain boots smelling of roses and mothballs leads to the kitchen, and we stop to notsee, notlisten, notthink about what is or is not in the house with us. Our persistent fear of intrusion butting against the persistent nothing that's there, and our persistent feeling that it will always be nothing, that the loneliness will deafen us to joy, should such a feeling still be possible. We walk through the long, open rooms, past kitchen and dining room and finally in the soft cushion of afghans and eyeless stuffed animals no longer seen, we bend to run fingers through the thick weave of carpet. Plastic fibers catch our nails as we lower ourself onto its bed. We think Fur and Counting sheep, and of his woman's forearm in an X-ray, tied at the wrist to the table so that when they order her favorite meal she can never quite reach. Can never taste it.

Our grandfather would say Patience is a virtue. He would say Good things come to those who wait.

Now, now, our grandmother would say, a mask of comfort over a plea to be quiet, to need nothing, to be more convenient. Now.

And we fall asleep, our hair weaving itself into the fibers that hold us in place.

When he sees us filling bags with rice and beans and grains we will forget in cupboards, dried and organized in jars more satisfying to observe than to open, he approaches, switching a gallon of milk to his left hand. He extends his right and says Hello, with a smile like he can't believe his luck, his name is David.

We do not reach out, and he wipes sweat from the jug on the lap of his dress pants. We wonder what day it is, if he's coming from work. The sun is up, but at this time of year the sun is always up, it seems, and we don't pretend to know how people pass the time.

I'm sorry I didn't introduce myself the other night, he reaches out again.

We take the hand because we haven't been trained to see an alternative. It is cool and moist and soft. It is confusing to be so close to a stranger. To anyone. To hold him. For a moment we think: This is what touch feels like.

We let go. You seemed busy, we say by way of an excuse. We cannot muster even a polite smile but remember the paid tab and add Thank you. For the drinks, I mean. A concession we know to make, but we do not wonder where such a lesson comes from.

Oh, David says, waving as if he'd made himself forget. As if he is as embarrassed of our impotence as we are.

It is quiet. Our fingers undulate on the bottom of the thin plastic bag so the desiccated bodies of seeds surround our hand in a loose dance held back by the frailest barrier of plastic. We forget to try to make it easy; we forget that it is uncomfortable to stand with a stranger. With us. We wonder for a moment who will eat what we buy with money we shouldn't spend as we imagine the satisfying pull of a razor across our skin.

We drop the bag into the red basket on our arm. It was nice to meet you, David, we've learned to say, and Be well.

His milk sweats onto his gray pants as he mumbles something, but we are already turning into the next aisle of cardboard boxes with cellophane windows, food looking out hungrily. Now, we whisper into their faces. Now, now.

We stand in front of a cooler, the low refresh rate of the bulb blinding. A child is singing ninety-nine bottles of beer, and when we reach for one, he sings ninety-eight. The mother smiles apologetically without knowing who her embarrassment is for.

Behind us, David says, That's a good one. We turn.

He nods to the bottle in our hand. Sorry, he smiles, and we think charm is something he practices in front of a mirror. That, he starts again, didn't go as I'd intended. I don't mean to be forward, but I'd like—he grows shy and, maybe in a hiccup of professionalism, extends his card—I was wondering if you'd like to get a drink sometime. The gesture is so cumbersome and unattractive that we recognize ourself in it, and there is the same unidentifiable current of sympathy, a nothing that pulls between us like a rope: We never expect him to die. How do the privileged suffer? Where do they learn sadness? How does such a person die?

Our cold distance has lost its bite or its meaning, and so we capitulate. Moving from one nothing to another is made easy by the appearance of this man.

We consider his persistence and our day and the days before this one, alone in the house, and maybe in a dare with some part of ourself we thought dead or simply without thinking or from too much day/night alone in the yellowed house, we move out of the way of the cooler and gesture to the many bottles with our own. It is a gauntlet thrown, and we do not believe he will pick it up. We are unsure if it is him or us that we are testing, and for a moment we are filled with the power we associate with sin. The incredible strength of controlling our own fall.

The light makes him look pale and glistens off the short graying hairs on the hard edge of his wide jaw. The hand, the card, hovers between us like a lost animal, and his look is one of notunderstanding. Oh, I meant anytime. I didn't mean tonight. I mean—he calculates and grasps—unless you're not busy? He watches the thick paper of the card as he flips it between his fingers and into the dark of his pocket.

We know we are inviting a man into the tight hallway of our home. We know the dry air and slick sweat of crossed thighs in the tunnel of hot rooms in July. We know the overhead kitchen light on the Formica counter and our grandmother's recipes and measuring spoons and juice glasses and cookie jars and doilies and the detritus of generations piled across the plasticky white as if anyone might use them.

And always in the other room our grandfather sits, reading seed catalogs, and our grandmother is sponging herself in the bath, and from our back on the thick rug, we listen to the whispered tick of the dying clock above our grandfather's fake leather chair, greenish and hard, and it would mean everything if he saw us, just over the fine print of catalog pages. Just once.

Now, we think and wait, watching his concentration so deep it seems a willful refusal to see us. Now, we think, as he turns a page. Now—but he never looks. Now, we wonder if we are really there. Now, now.

Even in that place, designed as if to quell sexual appetite, we expect David to expect sex because we have learned that this is a way to be seen. And in the white light of the grocery cooler there is a golden glint on his ring finger, and we expect him to absorb the mess he makes into the lap of his own life without yet knowing if we want him to.

If you want, we say. Already it is easier to defer to the desires of another. Already we are ready to disappear. It is familiar.

The child is bored and kicking at his mother's cart. She begins to roll away through a shiny spill, the wheel of the cart making an erratic pink trail across the tiles, flecked to disguise filth, and the woman is too distracted by the long list of her family's needs to see this other small mess. David smiles in a way that looks like laughing and opens the cooler door. David selects the same beer we are holding. The mother pushes the child away as he sings willfully and she gives in.

At the register, we become acutely aware of our purchases next to his. Of our prospective totals, the numbers like some evaluation of our worth rather than the cost of our groceries.

After paying, we wait just beyond the bagger as David's items are scanned. We look out the large windows onto the grocery store parking lot. We wonder if it looks like we're waiting for him. If we look like we're together. If we want it to.

How does one develop a taste for desire?

On our way out, we are confronted with the inelegant matter of transportation.

We had walked the three miles and intended to take a bus home, an attempt to fill the day. I could take you, David offers, and senses the new gravity of the situation. No longer a beer with someone new, but a young woman getting in the car of a stranger, the many possible outcomes, the worst of which always seems the most probable.

We remember that we want to die and think perhaps this will save us the trouble of doing it ourself.

Perfect, we say without the appearance of hesitation. He raises an eyebrow in surprise and leads the way to his car.

The radio is on at a low hum. Indecipherable murmuring accentuates the silence. We give directions. A left, a right. We look out the window at rubbish collecting by the curb and think Now. Now he will turn down that alley. Now he will reveal a gun and force our mouth over his cock. Now we will feel the swift slide of a bag over our head, a knife in our side. Now, now.

In any stretch of silence, David attempts conversation with So . . . , and ends his statements with an inflection to make it seem like a question: So. This is quite a walk to the grocery store?

We do not say we have nothing else to do. We do not say we find comfort in the deliberate organizational scheme of the grocery store's long aisles; we do not say that the familiar packaging ameliorates our anxiety, that commerce is a convenient stand-in for purpose. We say, It's a nice day for a walk. And eventually, This is it, here. The white one. We pull to the curb and get out of the car, noticing two ovals of moisture where our thighs have sweat onto the leather seat, and remember that we are not dead, but also that it's not too late.

The first thing we regret about bringing him to the washed-out yellow of the kitchen is the casual way he moves things—blue tin cups, duck-shaped salt and pepper shakers, napkin holder with three folded napkins—and puts them down somewhere else. We resent the rings his drink leaves on the wood of the kitchen table before he takes it up for security or courage, while a cardboard square printed with poppies sits embarrassed by its uselessness beside the wet circles.

This feels so impulsive, he says with a note of boyish adventure that surprises us.

We agree, turning to hide our irritation among the groceries as we put them away—we no longer remember why this man is in the house. He looks at the things, touches, picks up, moves, looks; always touching, like a child. To tend to his expectations now seems like an extraordinary amount of work.

We want only to lie on the floor, to stare at the familiar

peaks of the ceiling's plaster, to take our place among the useless objects, and we notice only then that David has not approached us, has not authoritatively taken our body in his hands. David differentiates between us and the plastic napkin holder or the 1972 regional fishing guide. We are not an abandoned thing baking in the house as we so often feel. He steps a few feet to the counter, and when we face him again he smiles, happy to be seen. It is a feeling we immediately recognize and long for.

The warm yellow glow of the hanging light paints him as a piece of furniture. Like the only thing that's been dusted. For a moment he takes on the golden sandy color of the brocade couch and curiosity stops us from resenting the time he is taking from us. We do not think about the other things we would not be doing if he were not protecting that small piece of counter, bit of floor. We feel nothing in the air. We are home *comma* and David is with us *period*

David grows uneasy in the silence and immediately fills it. I don't normally do things like this, he says to the gold flecks in the linoleum at his feet. He wants us to say Me too. He wants his presence to have meaning and for us to say You are special.

What do you do? we ask instead to force him to be a real thing. A thing that exists outside this New Life he is allowing himself to imagine. To separate himself from the dream of us in our house with the yellow light.

What do you mean? he asks, punctuating his question with a sip. For work?

For work, we say, to make it easy.

Finance, he replies as if unsure of the answer; not saying so proudly the thing we imagine he is trained to say proudly. What is credible in this strange environment, what would win our affection? Even we don't know.

Our response is a thought made from a feeling. Something as satisfying as *Oh*.

David's life becomes the puzzle of assumptions we've pinched together by frail nubs to explain the bright ironed blue of his shirt and careful haircut. In one seamless reversal of thought, we see ourself in his eyes. We see flesh in a loose lid of cotton, easy to open. We believe in that image instantly. When we are the man with money in our thirsty kitchen, we know we are clearing a path through the clutter of our life. Only a part of us grows sad with this inevitability because now we are that man too, and the power is intoxicating. As the powerful man, we see David, the salt and pepper, and the softness where his beer is going in that very moment. We feel the coarse hair growing on his shoulders moving all day against fabric, we make the muscles in his arms slack from disuse. When we are him, he is just David, and this makes him tangible, possible, bearable.

You know, personal finance. Retirement, things like that, he adds. And maybe it is our lack of understanding that tricks us into thinking this means anything. That he is accustomed to long days of wading through thick curtains of paperwork, of numbers, of solitary work, something familiar. A rare wisp of wind blows through gauzy curtains. We lean against the counter, facing him.

What else? we ask in the way people say For pleasure? We want him to wrap his damp fingers around the hot cords of our throat, to make the end easy for us. Now.

He says, I keep busy. His smile is knowing or suggestive, and though the comment seems vapid and empty, our rumpled dress heats translucent.

He is a stranger who looks at us from one eye to the next, and out of fear or pride we meet each gaze. His jaw softens out of a rehearsed, winsome smile and he reaches out a hand, moist with condensation, to run fingertips down the hot, dry skin of our arm.

And your wife? we ask. We are not satisfied to be the dust that covers everything. We must also be the termites and endless, exhausting summer days that make the dust. His hand falls to his side. The corners of his mouth move up, but he is not smiling.

I told you, I don't do this often.

How often is not often?

Never.

What is *this* that you never do?

Going home with a woman—we study the clouds of emotion as they move across his face and are edited—I didn't mean to imply . . . He watches the empty bottle as he taps it on the counter.

What does she do? we ask.

Lara? She's nice. And as if he doesn't remember saying it, or maybe for effect, he repeats: She keeps busy. When there is no reply, he explains: She's a therapist. He looks beyond us and bites the skin just inside his lower lip. He has withdrawn already into silence, somehow less arduous than it was moments ago when he still sought approval.

We reach out, imitating certainty. We rest a hand on his shoulder.

He draws us to him like a buoy to a man at sea, and we rest our head against him. It is both terrifying and nothing. We wonder only: Who is this?

For the time we stand this way, we think we could have

fallen on the dull sword of a butter knife, or died even more slowly in countless other ways: organizing the bookshelf by color, rearranging magnets painted to look like ladybugs on the freezer. We could have moved the to-do list of pills our grandmother tucked under the magnets' red wooden bodies three years ago to a less prominent place, could have watched our face grow sleepy in the matte reflection of the rusting bathroom mirror.

We feel him lift his head to look around, as if for the first time, because he needs something to fill the space between where he is and where he should be. This is an interesting place, he says. We nod into his chest and wonder if the grease from our face is soaking into his shirt. A lot of unusual stuff, he adds, looking for the answer to a question he doesn't know how to ask.

My great-grandparents built it, we say to the floor, our eyes open and comparing the slick black of his shoes to the pale toes of our feet, and below us the dark wet of an empty basement, blue-black and faraway in our mind from the pale gold of the house. And, we know, in that dark, a smaller house. The perfect size for a family of mice. The rooms built from scraps of the house that is its home. A house that dreamed itself. A small cardboard fantasy, forgotten and hidden out of view.

Looks like you haven't changed a thing. He says. Looks like my parents' house.

We are notlistening and distracted by the smell of his laundry detergent and we press ourself against him. He is a piece of furniture with a pulse. He is the bed we turn into a nest every night. We wonder if he can feel the prick of our nipples through his shirt. We suspect ourself of enjoying the company.

When he straightens, our hands drop to our sides as if they'd expected to be left empty all along.

His hands are warm and dry and hold each side of our face while his lips linger just at our hairline. His fingers slide back, behind our neck and into our hair; the hands hold the whole weight of our head, and he kisses our cheek. We want to be near the man we saw when we were the man with money, easy and confident and uncomplicated, because we are that man, or understand him best, or want to. We rest against his chest and he strokes our hair as it falls down our back. A finger is caught in a tangle for a moment and instantly we are angry for bringing him here, bored with the man who should be home, fucking the woman he loves. Or doesn't.

We pull away, say, Do you need to go? For a moment we believe the concern in our voice.

He looks at the oven clock, unoffended, and says, Yes/ He should get going/Here is his number/Call anytime. We have provided the excuse for him to undo his mistake, and we stop listening. We make it easy for him to leave us—easy for him and us. We walk with him to the front door, and he brushes our cheek with his thumb, kisses the top of our head.

Goodnight, David, we say. And he is gone. His body vanishes into the hazy, lingering light of summer. The house sighs with relief, and the air hangs itself in the still kitchen.

We sweep everything from the evening, bottles and David's number, off the counter and into the trash with a smooth and cathartic motion we wish to repeat over and over again. We move to the living room to be held up by the floor, suspended in the room as if adrift on a flimsy raft. We think only of David's faraway, milky dissatisfaction, of his eyes when he remembers that the man in the book will always die.

We neglect to lock the door behind us, and in the morning the house aches on our skin. We step outside to feel the cool sandiness of cement under our feet, and a thin trail like saliva catches our eye, shining in the morning sun, streaked across the stubbled surface of the ground toward the spines of dry grass. We wish for the snail's trick, to carry the house on our back, to be Atlas, glittering linoleum, the puzzles with missing pieces and bars of old soap, the rusted razors dropped into the wall behind the medicine cabinet and decades of dust woven into the thinning thread of the curtains—everything in our life in a constant state of rot—perched delicately behind us. The crisp air makes our hair stand on end, something in the day is clean and bright, the dark hallway stretches open behind us, the house, resting on a gentle slope, pulls us back like a lover, arms around the waist as if Come back to bed and Don't leave yet, and we think lips, we think David's lips on our neck, we think them moving from the tip of a shoulder to the back of an ear, we think lips and David could be there, we think about calling to him, the ten digits of him under new coffee grounds in the wastebasket. We think his mouth, we believe fully in the muted reds of that mouth, the washed away pink of his lips and the deep red flesh of his tongue, like a cunt, and in our mind we kneel over him, our cunt pressed to his mouth like offering communion, but we do not pull the soggy, thick card from the garbage: we want him to be easy, suddenly there. The door behind us sways in the morning's breath. Come, it says. Go, it says. We toe the dried trail of slime, arms crossed. The door sways. Come, it says, and we go inside. We turn the doorknob in our hand and return to the desert of the inside, the ocean of the day lapping always at the painted, flaking stoop behind us. The hollow wood of the door has a terrible new weight like a body, and we press against it, tired but warm in the residual heat of yesterday's sun.

Each day after David is marked by the number of days since he stood in the kitchen, claiming only one tile of ancient floor. We have taken out the trash and watched it carried away in the back of a truck that shakes the panes in the windows as it drives on. The thin sandwiches we make while standing in front of the open refrigerator fall apart in our hand, and we stare vacantly at the space across from us that feels new. David's absence is a new space. The air becomes a thing to touch and move through. We catch the lip of the counter with our fingernail absently. Over and over until the nail breaks close to its bed and becomes sensitive and pink. It flushes with the faintest crescent of blood. We sit in the bathroom, cutting our nails short like a man's, until they are tender—until it hurts.

We feel the weight of his lips on our forehead. We believe that if we turn around, if we scan the street through the lace curtain, we will see his silver sedan parked in front of the empty lot across the street, we will see his body waiting for our body in his nervous steps across the asphalt or quiet standing at the door.

To lose ourself is a new way to die, and when we wake at two and three a.m. with a sheet wrapped around our waist, we think he's found a way in and as a sleep-walker we let him. In this way, he takes more and more of the moments that used to be our own. The moments of hand-me-down reprimands, every *We don't do that*, and the tireless failures of youth. The arbitrary tests of self-discipline. How long can we hold our breath? How many years can we pass through quiet disapproval, how many years can we be haunted, how many years until the only voice that echoes in the house is the voice of the woman, the doctor, and her persistent death every day. It won't matter, we've decided, if the years won't come.

In the bath with just the light leaking in from the next room, we watch our hand in silhouette against the tile. The way the fingers move darkly through space. We think of the hands of a childhood friend. We once watched her clasp a ball before throwing it with all her might at a boy with a bat. We were stunned by the dark tan of her short fingers, the strength of them. She laughed easily with anyone, and we understood even then that it was incorrect to call her our friend because what we loved most about her was that she could not be contained or owned. But we were hers absolutely, because we required ownership to exist.

We loved and hated her for those strong, dark fingers.

David appears in the afternoon, Just for a moment, he says. He has soup and sandwiches in a paper bag from a deli downtown. We pull bowls and plates from the cupboards. We don't remember when we last used dishes. We set them out on a low wooden table in the kitchen, and we sit in brown faux leather chairs that roll along the uneven floor at any provocation.

Have you tried this place? David asks.

No, we say, still confused by his appearance, by his existence, by the necessity of a spoon. Everything is overwhelming, and for a moment, overwhelmingly beautiful.

We wonder about the stuff of him. The untouched tennis rackets and forgotten boxes under the bed with receipts and a college yearbook. In the same moment, we want him out of our mind. Want our own stuff out of our mind. Want the grandparents and preachers out of our mind. But the many things we have spent our life trying to escape are gone, and perhaps the world is so very overwhelming because it is entirely our own.

•

I wanted to clear the air, he says eventually, when the waxy paper flecked with turkey is folded and tucked under his plate. Things have been stressful lately and I got carried away. I worried when I didn't hear from you that you thought I'd been . . . unseemly. I'd still like to be friends.

We nod and smile and say reassuring things: Of course. Naturally. I understand.

But what does a friendship with this man entail? Will we be invited to Thanksgiving dinner? Bowling or backyard cookouts? Will his wife suggest we paint our nails together as she kindly tries to fix us? Or will it be a proliferation of stolen moments accented by forced chastity? We are bored with the limitations of the man. Of humanity. Of ourself. Of things, being what they are. Of spoons at lunchtime. Now. Now, now.

David stands. He has to get back to work. Was just stopping in. Call any time. His embrace at the door is perfunctory and embarrassed. He is proud of himself. He is ashamed of us.

When he leaves, we know that we will not, cannot, call him, and we lie on the floor to count the friends we've had. The last new friend we made was eleven years old. We were ten, and now she lives three states away and we haven't spoken in two years and even that, we suppose, is amazingly recent.

Three months before the end of the job, a woman confided that she planned to quit. We resisted the temptation to look around the room to see who she may have intended the secret for. We wondered if this was how friendships were formed in the workplace. Or perhaps if mutual malcontent was what brought people together. All of us are doomed, she added, filing her nails on a purple board. All those girls who work from home, she said, that was just to make it easier for them to let us go.

We look at the blinking cursor on our screen, then back to the nail file. Are you sure? We ask because we are supposed to ask, but we know that her certainty is why she is telling us. Because our presence signals a sort of death. Because talking to us is like talking to something already ended. Safe.

The plot of our days takes on a beige vacancy. The house is a hair shirt, and we have grown accustomed to being unable to scratch the itch. A lifetime of summers spent punishing ourself between bedroom and kitchen and living room floor has prepared us for the special ennui, though this time we have no one to blame but ourself.

While contemplating the crooked hang of a cabinet door, a feverish dissatisfaction compels us to leave the house. We will go for a walk. There is a hilarious practicality to it. To move one's legs. To be out of doors. To pass the time. The word *advisable* comes to mind, and when a sound comes from our throat, it takes full, long seconds before we identify it as a laugh.

You can't go alone, the grandmother says.

We pull on our shoes.

You can't leave the house like that. What will people think. They'll find your body in the lake. You need a man to take you/show you/protect you/tell you how to be.

We rest our head against the front door, waiting for it

to let us leave. And this is how we know. It is us—our fear and our shame and our pride—and no one else that paralyzes us.

We circumvent the cemetery on our way. Though we have been here before, on school field trips and walks after church and once on what might have been a date or might have been mutual existence in a specified place for a few hours after our class at the community college, the place feels new. The trees, though older than us, feel new. The painterly shades of green made by their overlapping leaves and the sound of families picnicking all seem incredibly new.

We round a bend and see a pulse of red. Someone emerging from the bushes? Climbing over a low stone wall? As we near, we see it is just a sweater. Forgotten or discarded. We realize we are holding our breath, have tightened the muscles in our neck, that we are clenching our jaw. We coach ourself that we are safe. That we will be fine. That it is daylight in a public park. That there will be sweaters. That there will be other people, and they will not hurt us. This involuntary reaction catches us off guard and makes us wonder if, despite how we feel on our back in the house with endless light, maybe we don't want to die. Or if biology will always betray us.

At home, by the window with an apple leaking unappetizingly over our fingers, mealy and inedible, we think David is out to lunch and imagine the fork he is lifting to his mouth, the careful way his teeth hold the pierced pink flesh. We create for him a gush of salty juice, we make his tongue control the meat as he teases it from the utensil. The muscles at his jaw work, food mixes with saliva, and he swallows. The body he eats moves through his own body and becomes him. The X-ray of his stomach in our mind shows the mass breaking apart like decaying, slowly, until it ceases to be a fish or a cow. It is only David's body.

In the evening, we imagine he is moving lovelessly through his wife. We remember her name and forget it. She is abstract. We think Simple. We think she is just lying there, and we think he is thinking of us, and when we answer the door, he is holding a bottle of wine like an excuse to be anywhere at all, and the sky is changing color and we step to the side as he enters.

I don't have to stay, he says quickly, as he follows us to the kitchen. I just thought I'd stop by. The silence that follows while we pick through a tangle of metal kitchen accoutrements floats between us like the long seconds of holding breath underwater and he fills the air like lungs: I hadn't heard from you and thought maybe you'd lost my number. He stops to watch as we slowly turn the key into the cork. And I didn't get yours.

He is already leaning against the counter in the same place, and we aren't compelled to invite him to sit, to stay. To do anything. We look over our shoulder while muscling the cork from the bottle, pleased that he is real, as if all this time he'd been an apparition. He looks confused or embarrassed. The cork is stained the deep red of death and skewered by the key. He is offering an excuse, an exit.

He waits, and when we do not ask him to leave, he asks how long we've lived here, where are we from?

We are (are we?) exactly where we've come from. But the man can't tell the difference. Even seeing us in the only context we can imagine, he would readily believe we were anyone, and while a lie is appealing for the possibility it presents to be new, to be other, to be not ourself for the brief duration of the lie, we are honest. This is the only place we've known.

He moved here from Florida. He says it with three syllables, Flor-i-da, and we wonder at the many shores it takes to make (someone) an island.

We press a glass into his hand and fill it to the top. We are relieved by his physical presence, that it silences his imaginary one.

He asks questions we don't know how to answer: How have you been?

We are unsure how we've been but remember that he stood in the same spot a week ago, and that we have looked at the David-shaped corpse of air as though it were a stain and worried that there is nothing we can do to remove the outside he has brought in, and the emptiness in us finally has a name. We remember running our fingers over cloth and opening doors and watching the white foam of toothpaste roll sadly down the drain. We remember the empty lot across the street coming into focus and turning to blurred background through the thick white rose-shapes of lace, we remember circling our own wet with a finger under the kitchen table, we remember drawing in the chalky dry windowsill dust: a series of stripes the width of a flattened pointer finger. We remember to say, Fine. And you?

Good, he says twice. Everything is good. Work is boring, but it's good. He seems like a person uncomfortable with uncertainty, eager to get past the obstacle of being learned.

In this flurry of common satisfaction, we fear that he is a counterfeit. That the David we have let grope at the stale parts of our imagination is really ourself in this man's face and dress shirt. That this man is only an imitation of the one we've created. We look around the room for an excuse to change the topic or make him change into the person he acted out the first time he stood in our house. Someone who, if he cannot see us, can at least be seen.

Artificial gold flecks every surface and we have nothing to say, but ask, What part of town do you live in? as we try to color him into a backdrop, like a doll in her house.

A wisp of cool air moves through the open kitchen window. The end-of-day light takes on an unnatural dark, tinted with pink. Mayfield, he says, and he becomes a man with matching luggage whose refrigerator holds only the sad glass jars of open condiments. Until we remember the wife, and her name, Lara, and the shelves fill with premade diet meals and flats of uneaten yogurt. We swirl the wine in our glass and smell it as if it will mean anything to us.

Do you like it? he asks with eyebrows raised for approval. I didn't know if you preferred red or white. I have a friend in California with a vineyard—David does not seem to know how to finish his own sentence—He sends me a few bottles every year. Maybe you don't even like wine?

It's nice, we say, swallowing most of the contents of the glass. Our tongue dries against the roof of our mouth. We take another mouthful and lean against the counter. In the first lull of alcohol spilling into our blood, everything becomes a waterfall: the sink behind us and the mess of David in our lives before us; moisture pools between our legs, the bottle in our hand again fills the glass, and immediately everything feels like drowning.

The light from the living room shines down the long open house; the color of everything is muted without warning until a snap of lightning illuminates our faces in ghostly white. We become aware of the angry rustle of leaves outside, and the smell of earth permeates the house.

We turn to look out the window: the neon of late summer days is sooty and gray with pregnant clouds.

David describes the optimal weather conditions and

soil pH for grapes, and he does not see that the world outside lifts like a wave. He does not hear the house groaning to hold us. It is the dry tomb that protects us from the slop of every path that starts at the door. He tries to keep the conversation afloat and reaches for our attention, anything to anchor the moment: What do you do?

Yeah, we say, distracted for the old wood of the window sills and floor concealed under tile and the years of filth that have baked carefully into the curtains and carpets, perfectly preserved. We should close the windows, we say as rain begins to pour off the roof in thick sheets.

It'll be fine. David places a hand on our arm to stop us from moving away. The breeze feels nice, he says. In another flash, David's face is overexposed, sharp contrast where bones make tents of his skin and compose the graves of his eyes. What sort of friend, we wonder again, will this man be?

The electricity flickers and the house goes foggy. In the thick light we can't make out the purple stain of his lips, just the shadow of features against a pale backdrop. We look from the shadow of his brow to the dark curve of his mouth. Our lips and thumb tingle numbly. The small circle of his palm moving to our waist is fire where the cool air blowing through the house turns us into the flesh of something plucked or skinned. Raw. We lean forward, and in the next stroke of lightning his eyes are pools. We imagine our face as the endless black of silhouette against the window, a shadow puppet, and the desert of our tongue finds the cool wet of his mouth.

Our hand sliding across the counter knocks our glass, purchased at a yard sale, ancient even then, to the floor. Despite the press of David's mouth we see for a moment behind our closed eyes our grandmother, the image bright with the artificial glow of something remembered, like the saturated color of old film. We see her hesitant collapse into the rolling chair, her resigned free fall rehearsed for decades, the glass placed delicately on the counter. The milky memory even of neighbors, innumerable neighbors ago, trapped, then shattered in the thin edges of glass.

David pulls away to apologize for what we've done, to say Let me clean that up—grasping at the opportunity to take it back, to leave innocent, to run to Lara. Glass and a blood-red spray glint off the tile. The wine sits on the plastic floor in beads, pooling together and running over the uneven surface.

We toss a kitchen towel printed with geese wearing bonnets over the mess and rest against the lip of the counter. It will be fine, we say, leaning toward him.

The house whines as its joints swell. David's body is heavy with reservation and guilt, but he takes fistfuls of our flesh as if he can carry it away with him. His short hair pulls between our fingers. The great suck of our lives opens in the pit of our stomach and we know that we do not know why the man is here but that we want him to stay not forever but for this moment, and to carry this moment around for whatever forever looks like. You should be ashamed, our grandparents say, and we are. It feels like being alive.

We lick the soft shell of his ear and he presses his hips into us. He pins us to the counter. For a moment the danger is not doing something wrong, to Lara—we picture her turning the pages of a magazine in soft lamplight—to the voices that still scold from every rocking chair, but to ourself. We will not be distracted by the long, straight slope of her nose or the labial pink of her lips. Her existence is the distraction, her absence the thing we grope between us.

Lara must be privileged and boring because we are too lazy to give her humanity. If she were an interesting person, a good person, even an undeniably real person, we would have no one to hate but ourself, and that would feel like starting all over again.

He becomes gentle, thumbing our nipples absent-mindedly. He is already pulling into his long driveway, the simple elegance of his life falling into place. He says something we cannot hear until, confusingly, the skirt of our grandmother's dress bunches at our waist as his hands search for our body in the fabric.

Our mouth to his, his hands pull down our underwear, pull our hair, unfasten his belt, and his fingers slide inside of us. We are overwhelmed by the many places he occupies at once, stunned by this omnipresence. David unbuttons our dress deftly to suck our breasts like a child, his head cupped in our hands. His tongue circles a nipple slowly and in our stillness we feel the shame of his infidelity coupled with gratification in our own abetment. Our hands move over David's body in fear, in longing, in confusion at the new absence of loneliness. We take his cock in our hand and meet the litany of silent objections hiding in the walls in an even rhythm with his hips. He pulls away and returns, pulls, thrusts, pulls until just out of reach, he returns, he slides between our legs, and we freeze with fear we haven't felt long enough to identify. We say condoms, he doesn't have one (why would he?), he's been married for fifteen years, he says, what are we worried about? We don't say: everything. We can not, he offers, his cock still sliding along the lips of us, his tongue pressing into our mouth. The instant is prolonged as if forever. It is the infinite moment just before we pull the razor across the skin and know we could stop but won't. We open our mouth to say Wait, but then the cock slides into the wet and we are quiet/surprised/embarrassed and David does not notice. He is inside of us, and there is no escape or better version. There is just this. There is just David inside of us as we stare at the blue designs painted on the wooden hutch behind him. We swallow the terrifying aftertaste of the self-destructive tendency. Our hips roll in quiet motions of desire, as if pretending it isn't happening, as we had always done it, alone, unthinking, waiting for it to start and finish, as if it could happen without our knowing, rubbing swollen clit through our own swamp against him.

He braces himself against the counter, and he breathes down onto us like fog. We consider that pleasure could be a noble pursuit. We consider that we asked for it. We consider that we want it.

We do not want to own him, we do not want to take him from Lara, we do not want to owe him forever for leaving his wife, we do not believe that he will. We choose to believe in the moment's want, the bursting emptiness between everything to fill with David's shape, because it gives the impression of agency. The emptiness grows and holds its breath like drowning; it washes us in a rhythm we meet in even pulses until Lara's flesh grows hot between us, her body so learned in his body that the guilt makes our/her cunt desperate to commit the sin more completely. We pull him deeper into us; he bends to lick the sweat from the wells made of our clavicles.

He moves rapidly, one arm around us to grip the counter, the other wrapped around our shoulder—pulling us/her down onto him. We wonder with terror if he is allowed to be there, as if there is someone outside of ourself we could ask for permission, and our fear makes us come, and the guilt is deafening. Our pleasure springs from the disapproval raining from generations of Good Christian Women and from Lara, and from David. I'm going to come, he says, as if realizing the possibility for the first time.

He shudders into us and hangs limply on our body. Even as he grows soft and slides out of us, he leans into us as if he cannot stand on his own. Then, as if remembering (Lara), he straightens and pulls away, his pants still embarrassingly at his ankles. A trail of white crawling down our thigh leads to the dark of our insides and reflects soft light filtering through dark, dense air. David bends to pull up his pants; he fastens them and leans toward us, kisses our cheek. I guess I got carried away, he says. I hope that was alright?

I'm fine, we say, disoriented, filled with alarm without direction. There is only the sharp contraction of our heart that means we are wrong. Bad. Dirty. Wrong. And what would be the benefit of saying that he took more than we were prepared to give? We fit our arms back into the holes in our dress, buttoning it and smoothing it down over our thighs. We suffer sin without believing in sin. The weight of disappointment grows as we rehearse the lineage of our wrongdoing until we unfeel David's guilt pooling beside us, his own torment a question mark hanging from his neck.

In the vacant air, David reaches for whatever he is reaching for. The thing that will quiet his own nameless longing. He picks up his glass and taps it against the counter. He asks, Are your grandparents still living? He is looking anywhere but at us, and he will talk about anything but the thing he has done with us.

We say no, but could mean yes. They both died in the last few years, we say. He apologizes for their deaths, with Sorrys empty for his inability to have changed anything. And when he says his parents are still living in For-i-da, we see them suffering in a black, open future matching day for day their past while our own parents will drive forever in the phantom history of a car accident, a memory out of context, as if it belongs to someone else. As if it were true.

It sounds as real when we say it to David as when our grandparents told the lie to us. A car crash, statistically probable, but so is the grandparents' decision that the parents were unfit. No funeral, no grave, no urn, no black armband. And the grandmother said, at her own end in the shocking cold white of the hospital room, some clarification before it could not be given: They are dead now, by the way. And then: You were better off.

And so we accepted a new mourning, but for what? For parents already dead to us. And were we dead to them? And the questions (Did they come for us? Did they care? Did they want us? Why were we taken away?) seemed unspeakably obvious when the only person who could answer them was dying herself, and might have said anything.

The quiet shifting from one life to another felt even to our child self like a miscalculation. And yet we can't remember a home before this one, not now. Now, now.

All I know, we say, is my mother's name was Ruth. We do not say we learned this by way of threats—Don't do that; you'll end up just like Ruth. Ruth, less a person and more a symbol of evil, of failure. Like us, we think. Like us now, we think. Dirty like us, bad like us now. Now, now, now—

It is easier for David to believe a nothing-car moving as a star through space, displacing matter and glass, and we tell it as it has been imagined to us, without our curiosity disrupting the bright noise of collision. A story we rub into the fabric of brittle dresses hanging in the closets, without the will to find a different answer and without anybody to ask.

David accepts responsibility in I'm sorrys for our whole past, entombed and disintegrating in the shape of tatted doilies on end tables.

Sweat crawls slowly down our back, but the hair on our arms stands on end. In the cover of dark and gooseflesh, we ask, and: No, David sighs. I don't have kids. He's quiet and the question is wrong, too soon, and it hangs in the unreal place between us where we unknow ourself in relation to this new man and exhaustion and uncertainty. He says after a moment, It's probably too late now.

The house takes in these new unnamed faults, filling the cracks between poorly fitted pieces of counter and narrow passageways behind furniture that cannot be pressed flush against the wall, the voices of our grandparents behind closed doors, whispering to each other while we choke our breath in the deep, soft mattress of our mother's old room. We make an island in the sea of tiles and listen for their holy guidance in the emptiness we've always moved through: Nothing is right for a young woman to do/say/think/be.

And what would Lara think?

Are you worried? we ask, though the question feels false and strange, like wearing our grandfather's slippers to the mailbox. And perhaps in the same way, we expect only the eventual changing color of bills or the necessary relocation to a new existence. We turn to look at him. We notice his body in a new way and wish to see the body, its ridges and nooks and uninterrupted landscape like dunes in moonlight. We wish to be comfortable.

He smiles/shrugs. Are you? he almost laughs, and maybe things could be easy/fine. We are in disbelief at our own presence in this moment.

I don't know you very well, we say finally. I want to understand, we say, why you are not with your wife now.

Exhausted, David exhales a long, damp breath to join the moist air around us, to be taken back to the sky and made rain in another city, as if from dust to dust, ocean to ocean. Lara's mother is in the hospital in Denver, he says. She went to be with her, and I had to stay for work.

How rude, we think, for the mother to wait so long. Until Lara is an adult and must confront fully the impending absence. You do not worry that everyone you know and love will die when everyone you know is dead.

David says into the wet air, I'd be lying if I didn't admit that I wanted to see you. I meant it when I said I wanted to be friends. You seem—he looks for the word—intriguing. He adds quickly, seriously—But I didn't expect this.

What did you expect? We try to see ourself through his eyes again, try to see the sum of us, a girl at the bar, the house, a body. Perhaps to him we are something outside of life—a mirage, the glinting of semen and wine and rain, all figments, all fool's gold under a quick cold stream of old laminate.

I mean, he explains to the flecked counter, and then deflates against the edge of it, defeated: I don't know. Maybe I thought I had more willpower, or that I didn't really need something else even though I feel all day—we see him moving from office to document to home to table to bed—that I need something else. That meeting you and seeing you again would be nothing. That it could keep happening by accident.

He reaches out, and we rest our head in the hollow place between the shoulder and chest of the man. He half wraps us in his arm, fingers making a light trail of touch on our back. The rain falling slowly, suspended in a veil outside the window, we stand separately together, silently filling and emptying each other with our selves and needs and impressions.

He says with importance, Yesterday was our anniversary.

This means nothing to us, but he asks, Do you feel guilty?

It hangs like an apple, a test, and we feel him lift his head to look down at us. Our heart swells and hardens in our chest, full of the electricity of our shame. If we feel guilty, we are weak, and if we don't, we are cold.

No, we say simply, because the date is not what makes us guilty. Lara is so much a part of what we have fucked that even when we build her into a woman easy to hate, she is still watching, feeling, analyzing the way we touch and move against his body, and we feel the inherent child's guilt of theft. We make the happy wife/woman; the educated, responsible woman; the tolerant or thoughtful wife; the easy or melancholy woman; the hungry wife/woman who perhaps wants to be swollen with this man like a nesting doll, a flesh full of seed to become flesh full of seed—we make her a fool.

David's chest rises and falls with the cooling air in the kitchen. Lost in his own guilt, his breaths all What have I dones and Who is this womans, he's not sure if he should extract himself in quick movements, running from the house always when in his mind he comes to the house to stand this close, to fuck, to be new in something, to remind himself that he is alive by notdying in the still, perfect air of these rooms. But maybe also he thinks it is just as right, the same to never go back/to collect his things/to leave a note. To stay, to move away, to learn someone else, to be a monk or crazy or a whore is the same thing when he stands in this notreal space—though it is for the moment the real space, and that other, with the wife, faraway and illusory like a dream of floating and waiting, always waiting with reluctant trust to be caught, but expecting to fall through.

David leaves and we are choked with the fear—not that we cannot live without the man, but that the man cannot live without us. That he will die on his way home, that at the end of the story all men die, and as quickly as the fear comes it goes because no one will tell us if he is dead. He is limited to the walls of our memory. He lives and dies with us.

There is a melancholy exhaustion in the walls when we wake up alone. We touch between our legs, feeling at once satisfied, like a mother watching a child sleep, and sick on the choking knob of grief growing inside us. We run a finger around the hole still covered in sex, and the guilt comes back a comforting blanket.

Our body mourns David, we want to see him both never and immediately, for the sharp hairs on his face to rub raw the skin around our mouth, the rhythm/weight of a body on and filling ours; that body waking up next to his wife and us plagued with our own litany of condemnation: We are hurting someone. And maybe: We are hurt.

As we go about enduring our day, we discover there is no way to sit that does not remind us of David, the house creaks and swells with the moisture in the air. We recite the dispassionate voice of the woman's dictation *comma* and recall watching as other women's misfortune would grow in our typed words *period* Through the impassive veil of the woman's voice, we hear the tick of the clock. The refrigerator hum. The moan of the wooden boards. Rain continues to fall grayly, streaking the windows in trails lit up in silver streams from the inside by dusty lamps.

The next day: Remembering broken ankles and the tiny bones of children's hands is interrupted by his knock at the door. He stands empty-handed in the cloudy noon colors. Our body stirs into riots of anger and lust in a thin film of manicured indifference, but we smile involuntarily before it's too late and he laughs: I would have called, but I still don't have your number.

We shrug. Don't you have to be at work? And he is

hurt so easily we say: I'm just surprised to see you—do you want to come in?

I don't have to; you're probably busy, he's been trained to say, and we: I have a moment.

He lingers on the stoop, glittering with moisture as dark spots form and grow around him/on his clothes as fresh rain starts. Come in, we say, swinging the door open, and he enters. In the dark hallway, he steps close to tuck a strand of hair behind our ear and kiss our head like a father. Like what we imagine a father might do. We follow him to the kitchen, so bright against the outside, and for the first time he continues. Walks past the stain he's left on his memory of that room, and enters the dining room, separated from the kitchen only by the counter yet a different world.

Do you work from home? he asks, as if it has only just struck him that we are always here, always available, always a part of this house. When we shake our head no, he asks, What do you do, with the detached fascination of an anthropologist, a college student at a museum. Under the curiosity, a note of suspicion.

Medical dictation, we lie, and think only of its ending. Until recently, anyway.

Hm, he says, and we hate that we have insinuated our failure. That we have shown him anything. That we are not easy, a nice girl at a counter, in an office, at a restaurant. Not the girl who can smile at a stranger in a bar—he does not remember meeting us. We were never there, not the woman who did not want him, did not want to be anything for him. And in his eyes and in the eyes of someone so comfortable with themselves, the house seems to hunch, seems to grow old in front of us and we know instantly each growing water stain and crack in plaster and leak to the basement; we taste a creeping desperation more bitter than guilt.

I'm considering other options, we say. The words are empty and offhand, like a clump of dirt thrown onto a casket. His curiosity has been appeased, though, and he accepts this without question, and we are filling with disgust for our own simple inadequacy and perhaps hurt by his lack of curiosity or concern. He looks at us as if for the first time and we remember: We do not know this man.

We wonder what made us desirable to the man? What has made the wife tiresome? Is it simply her wifeliness? For what would the man leave the prison of his own making? And would he not simply find, once he'd left, that his backwards glance is not looking into the cell he'd escaped, but through bars of yet another prison?

He would leave her for nothing.

Then for nothing the man is in our home, and the knowledge makes us resentful.

But are we not more in love with the plastic covers over the dining room chairs than with this man? Who are we to judge?

The sex is still between us and our sweat still clings to the air, the rain casts the same pallor through the house, but we glow with the house's sandy desert light and he moves to our body because, now familiar, it is the easiest place to hide. He wraps his arms around us and says into our hair: I couldn't stop thinking about you.

And though we, too, have thought only of David, of his presence or absence, we say nothing. Only imagine David in a building made of glass that reflects the sky it imposes upon, thinking through the stream of rain down walls of windows, about spilling us across his desk. As in a mirror across town, we think of David unwrapping us in the kitchen and moving through us in the bed. He is tied in the tangle of our sheets and driving up to the end of the sloping lawn in each long, lonely tick of the loud wall clock. Afraid of being taken, of our own great desperate longing, of the loss of everything around us: I want—we say into his ear without looking into the terrifying wells of his eyes, like a child asking for something she cannot have, with shame we try to say To be your whore, but cannot make those words form in our mouth, the performance of it, and say instead—to do what you want me to. It feels like the tines of rusted tools in the basement, the shape of the thing, but useless. He is flattered/aroused/scared. I want to be treated carelessly, we say, running the tip of our tongue along his neck. We make it so there is nothing he can do to us that we do not want him to do, nothing he can take that we have not given.

We understand that we are making these concessions not because the man is strong, but because we've been told that we are weak. We do not want to shame him, but to shed our own shame, and so when he came back we opened the door, and when he touches us we will open our body and we will make ourself the executor of the will we've chosen among two poor options.

David swallows but says nothing. His hand slides over our breast and up to rest by our mouth, the thumb following the outline of our lips, then pressing between them, our eyes on his eyes until Lara is pushed outside of us, the thumbprint rubs on the sharp edges of our teeth and the wet muscle of our tongue works against him like our sex. We lower to our knees open his pants lick the shaft as it grows, and in the heavy relief of regret, we suck, hungry to owe him nothing and take with each long pull of the mouth our debt for being wanted. In the white rush of come to throat, his hand pulling hair/our head back/our eyes on his/as the come chokes us, David is for the moment the debtor.

David does not ask again for our number. He comes and goes as he pleases.

Is there a word for finding pleasure in fear—would Lara say the strength of these feelings isn't love, but terror?

And once on the playground when we corrected a class-mate about the true day of the Sabbath, explaining to them only pagans worship on Sunday, we felt a smug superiority for our membership in the correct religion. And with the pride came enormous fear that no one else knew it was all a lie.

When David leaves we lie on the bed and move the tight muscles in our lips, tonguing the metallic dents left by our teeth. The first drop startles us, a confusing tap at the end of the bed. We see particles of moldy dirt splash on the tattered rug. We look up, a brown ring grows on the ceiling, and David becomes the hum of the refrigerator buried under everything, the single drop drowns our thoughts of him, we burn with helplessness at the intrusion.

Surely, we say in the calm voice of the woman, there is a logical solution *period*

Surely we have been negligent, our grandparents remind us of our Christian duty to cleanliness and Godliness. Surely we know better. Surely they raised us better than this.

When we place it under the leak, the pink plastic trash can makes a hollow tap with every drop. Each echo resounds of the bills that will collect. Even the flicker of gold on the foggy memory of David's left hand is no longer a liberating, but now a fresh, suffocating end. The bulge of grief and the unstoppable progress of sadness that chokes us like David pressing into the back of our throat.

Backlit images of X-rays filter through the imagined lengths of rope we consider tying first to our neck and then the metal bar of the closet. The house weeps from the inside into the trash. Lightning lights the house like the beginning of the universe: the womb of our home fills with an artificial brightness, but lacks the strength to stop the mess of the outside coming in.

We curl into the nest of the bed, wrap the house around our cancer of sadness. Crying contorts our face into an ugliness that we cling to until the sobs and muscles moving involuntarily disgust us. Gasps first caught in our throat drown in the salty swamp of the pillow until, nestled in our own shallow cave of pain, we fall asleep exhausted, without David or thoughts of David or even the desire to be consoled.

Who can lift the burden of sadness from us? Not David. Nor can we take David's. No matter how great our capacity for pain, we cannot carry his, like a cumbersome parcel, dutifully to the grave—the only future we trust. Though we understand death is only an easy solution for the already dead, we can't imagine how else one elegantly exits the unbearable reality of the present moment.

We develop a desire: escape. We want to fall through the trap door of our life to something else—something that will be better because it is different. Though we see David's flaccid arms, we want him to catch us when we come out on the other side. No—we correct ourself—we want him to want to despite his inability.

Around the tub is a clutter of half-used shampoo bottles a decade old, Old Spice, bubble bath, crackled slivers of soap dried to their dishes. We put it all out of focus. To our blurred vision there is nothing as far as the eye can see.

We drag the razor across our arm without pressure, just an apathetic curiosity. Pale hairs yield to the blade. We run it along our stomach, our hands, our face. Places that once appeared hairless grow a dull bald sheen. This is our body, we say to ourself. The body is a temple. A temple is a house of God. God is a construct, we counter, invented to explain earth sciences and pacify the existential torment of the human experience.

And yet we feel no better.

Sometimes I'm sad, we admit to him one night in comforting lamplight during a visit when we are still new/don't say: every day I want to die. And he puts his arm around us. This is what the man can do; this is all he can do.

Are we dishonest because we are embarrassed, or because we do not believe he will care? Should he?

Don't ask questions, for God requires us to have faith like a child. Don't touch, for your body is a temple. Don't be that way, who will want you? Be good. Be a good girl.

When David whispers That's a good girl, ride my cock like a good little slut, we do as we always have and obey.

David never calls at midnight to say:

There are no numbers to call and no distant voices traveling detached from our bodies and nothing outside of us can say I miss you. or How are you? or I'm thinking of you./Are you touching yourself? And we do not say aloud to ourself that this will make it easier later, when it is over, so we will not be tied to the man by phone lines, we will not know the manicured lawn in front of his house, the proximity to favorite restaurants, the benign good taste of his life; it is good to keep him out of reach. And David does not say it will make it easier to keep from his wife when she returns, though it will, and he does not invite us into the clean luxury of his existence. Instead, David appears on the cement step on the seventh day of Lara's trip, like a private Sabbath, holding a paper bag. I brought some things for dinner, he says walking in. Have you eaten already?

No, we say, confused by the comfort of pretending like children to be man and woman. When he begins to fill the dented pots with water and turns the gas on under them, we know to rub with our fingertips on the dry fabric of his shirt as he says it's a good day: the twenty dollars in a pocket and work and now he's here and he says that we make a good day. And our day, our existence as it crumbles around us is painted over in more pretending: that we should fill his glass; we should read the lines of his palm with humor and good fortune; we laugh when he says, I can be generous, as if: I can make you/this easy. We do not correct him that it is us who is giving so freely what he is looking for. That he will never be generous with what we need. We don't want to be saved, just seen, to be real, okay, enough, but the water boils over, the white foam spill distracts him so that when he lifts the lid and steam fogs the clock and small window that looks out to the front door, we breathe deeply to forget as if it is the same as forgiveness, and when he replaces the lid he begins to pull new items from the paper bag: oil, spices—and we imagine these things lining the shelves in the clean hush of a remodeled kitchen, we imagine Lara by the stove, a good wife at the stove—and we say, I have all of these things. Laughing that he thinks we do not live in this house, or that we exist from nothing, but when we remember the wilted produce in the crisper drawer and the blank stare of the shelves every afternoon as we try to sustain or distract ourself, we wonder if he is right, if we do not know ourself at all. If we have never been seen because we aren't here.

I didn't want to make any assumptions, he says offhandedly, running a hand down our back, and we shiver under the touch. We pull a thread of pasta from the pot and throw it against the wall for the first time since childhood, and it sticks in the shape of a cursive S. He removes the pot from the heat, and with its steam rising from the sink where he has drained the water, he holds us. The lip of the sink pressing into our low back, a cooked smell surrounds us like a shower and we cannot distinguish his body pressing against us from the house he presses us against. And after dinner, on the couch he says again: I didn't expect this. We wonder again what This is, but smile instead, running our fingers down his long thigh until the friction on our fingertips feels like a burn.

Why us? we want to ask, but say instead: Have you ever broken a bone?

Of course, he laughs and extends the fingers of his left hand. There is an unusual twist to the index finger so that it appears to be permanently pointing to the right.

What happened? we ask, taking the hand in our own to examine it more closely as if we might see under the skin and hear the doctor's voice describe the broken parts of David aloud so we don't have to pull them from him.

Oh, it got smashed with a baseball bat.

You played baseball?

No—he seems reluctant to continue—well I did, in elementary. T-ball, he says and laughs.

But that's not when you broke it?

No.

We watch the tightening of his jaw, and the lines at the corners of his eyes deepen as he knits his brow. It is a restrained expression, like puzzling at a difficult math problem to avoid the smart of admitting you don't know. *I* didn't smash it, he says finally. My dad did. It was an accident, but he was angry, and he was often angry, so it's always been hard to be sure. His face relaxes. It's complicated, he says dismissively.

No, we say, it's not. It's just hard.

Later, he presses our face into the mattress and we stand on our toes to meet his hips. And while we fill with a metallic dread, we don't imagine that in the inevitable, excruciating end, he will stay. He is hers. Behind us he is a figure lost in the corners of our eyes, a man already disappearing even when we are closest. He presses the back of our head, our breath catches in the folds of old blankets, he pulls our hair so the breath is squeezed out in thin cords of a neck stretched taut. And through clenched teeth: You like that. And we remember that now we are his, so we like it. We remember we can be generous and give readily so that nothing can be taken from us. But we say only Oh, God.

The red sweater is matted from the rain. Someone has hung it over an informational plaque describing native plants. We imagine their reluctance to touch it. Someone else's clothing, so personal, and left to be sullied by the weather for an indeterminate length of time. Has the owner of the sweater been back since the time of their loss? Have they also seen it and been too ashamed to take it home? Were they an out-of-town guest, on a walk with their sister, and now are they home catching a chill and wondering about their sweater? Are they thinking about it right now? Can they see it through our eyes? If we think of each other at the same time, are we connected even if we can't be together?

On the way home we go by the cemetery. We visit the plots of our grandparents that once looked like twin beds of unestablished sod against the endless carpet of green. We still can't quite believe that they've moved. That their bodies are not shuffling through the long house, but are here, awaiting resurrection. In this politely manicured expanse they seem at a loss for words. Perhaps it is a sense of propriety that keeps them from expressing indignation, resting, as they are, in the Lord's waiting room. Or maybe it is a fear of appearing unfit for entrance into the Heavenly Kingdom. Or maybe it is we who require all of their earthly possessions to animate their ire, like the tools of a well-cast spell.

Each evening Lara is away, David comes earlier and leaves later each morning so that the days with him grow longer, the very small hours of night an ocean wide forever so we can take more of him into ourself before she is back and David tells her, we see so clearly in our mind the way he will say, kissing her eyelids: I love you. Then: But—and his hands in her hair and the weight of her, the baby body weight of her head resting in his hands, as easy to crush. And he walks out to this, another life. Even if we chant each night that we are some temporary other existence—Lara surely knows why people behave this way, has read many books on the subject, and she knows why people leave to see what else—we can still see him arriving in our life like a ship. We can so easily mistake his persistence or desperate reaching for devotion.

Lara, with all her knowledge and training, could give a lesson on what is wrong with the man, and with us, and prescribe a pill or routine. And her? Why does she stay?

•

And what object lesson do we give with our presence in the man's life, in Lara's life without her knowing? Just the objects themselves, the miscellaneous articles in drawers and shelves stacked and corners meticulously filled with all the treasures piled and forgotten. We could teach the ancestry of objects preserved as a museum to the absence of love, to tenderness stored more faithfully in hairpins collected in mason jars than in our lineage of fallible hearts.

In the morning he dresses for work and we watch from the mess of floral sheets as he tells us about the appointments for the day and the way a coworker reminds him of a friend from graduate school and how he is always stopping himself from being overly casual with her, since she seems so familiar. We smile at the story and watch as a wave of suspicion crests in our mind. We remember the job's quick ending, the parents' absence, how easy it is to find a solution to the problem of us. That we are replaceable, so we will be replaced.

Roses on a yellow background interrupt our limbs as they stick out of the bed. When we reach for him, he comes back smiling. For this moment—when he is still buttoning his shirt and looking down at the button with his mouth in a frown like a child working out the mechanics of a jacket—we reach out and he comes, and though we know he will leave, for the moment he is here and his presence is a quiet affirmation that we, too, exist.

Were we always alone?

There were schoolmates and sleepovers, but even in these memories it is the ear of an invisible friend we whispered our secrets to. Grandfather reading quietly in his chair, grandmother at the stove or by quilts well-intended and always half-finished. Sometimes visitors sat with the grandparents at the table and talked quietly, endlessly.

Kids would say Your parents are so *old*. And we would clarify, *Grandparents*. And they would ask, Why do you live with your grandparents? And we would say Because my parents are dead, and find pleasure in their uneasy apologies and slow backing away.

It was the eyeless fake dog perched on our dresser we fell in love with first, then blankets, and hat pins and vases, rusted simple machines in the garage, and the smarting of a rubber band against our wrist. And later, clippings of celebrities from magazines who might understand us based on certain melancholy expressions, and later still, whole characters from books and the color and smell of the paper where they lived, and the moments we spent together, and finally, nothing. Just a bland hunger that persists no matter what we feed it.

When the notice comes from the city, we open the garage and climb through the spiders to remove the push mower. Even in our youth when we resented the obligation, we appreciated its simple design and straightforward mechanics. As we wheel it into the sun, we see the blades are rusted and fantasize the catch of skin on rusted metal. Tetanus. Dismemberment. This is as far as our imagination will take us. We push the machine across the cracked driveway to the lawn and begin. It is more difficult than we remember. We strain up the slope and allow the heavy blades to pull us when we turn to go back down. Though it is forbidden by the grandfather who comes out to check our work, we change directions and pull along the side of the slope creating an inconsistent pattern in the uneven grass. He tells us to oil the machine, to sharpen the blades, to maintain. We push across the hill. The damp grass sticks to our shoes. Our hair, stomach, back, groin, legs are wet with sweat. Neighbors we don't know say hello. We nod in reply. There is pleasure in the strain. We know our back will hurt. We know we will lie in a cold bath with a beer. We know we will be reminded of the effort tomorrow and are reminded of David and marvel that we have not thought of him until now.

As we sweat and push, we think of the pastor telling a joke:

What was Boaz before he married?

Ruthless.

We see still the vision of our grandparents contracting bitterly in on themselves and how we formed the word in our mouth: Ruthless. And whispered it to ourself all that night like an incantation.

Moments with David are episodic and, because we do not know each other, seem to float without context:

What did you do with all your time before you came here? we ask, naked in bed beside David's body. He laughs the way he laughs when he is uncomfortable. He laughs often.

I guess I went home. I don't know what I did there—eat, sleep. Read sometimes, but not as much as I used to. Talk to Lara.

Who knows what happens in the liminal hours? we say, as if it were a joke.

What did you do before me? he asks with unusual interest.

What do you do is simply: How full is your life? Mine is empty, will you fill it?

And so what do we say with our own enthusiasm for the man? Make me in your image, make me wealthy, comfortable, secure. Make me someone with someone.

•

We do not say: pluck the hair from our legs one at a time. Nor: practice drawing exact circles with the nubs of empty pens, bite every piece of fruit in the dish and leave the rest to rot, stare at the shelves of the refrigerator and feel a quiet vibration in its eerie light, lick the sharp new hairs that grow back after we've cut them off our arms, braid the short shag of the polyester carpet, hold our breath in the tub, or walk to the cemetery down the road to lie on our grandparents' graves. The only place where they're quiet.

I like to read, too, we say. I've started walking to the park.

We do not tell him about the sweater, and the withholding makes it ours.

The rough grating of synthetic fibers under us as David pushes us down burns away skin and the vestiges of our isolated history. That once: between the innocence of our carpet-bound adolescent despondency and David's blind destruction of our memories of that time was the burn of a short brown carpet against our back and the blue flicker of a movie on the boy's turned face. A few rooms away his parents sleeping, and a few blocks away the window to our room propped open, and after just a few moments his quiet pulling away and only: This was a mistake. Under David, we stare at the stippled texture of the ceiling and swallow our shameful need. That pitiful and persistent desire not to be a mistake.

At night we dream of wolves. Their hunger forces us to admit the embarrassing: that we want to be special, exceptional. We want them to spare us, we want to be revered by something wild and beautiful. But when their teeth burrow into our flesh, we force ourself to watch. Do not look away, we say in the dream. This is what you wanted.

We open our eyes in the creamy ruffle of bedspreads and feel the disquiet of danger at the base of our neck.

David says one evening after a long silence that people are dependent on one another. We look up from our book, from where we rest our head on his knee, and he says, closing Nietzsche around his thumb and lowering the book to the arm of the couch, Like sentences.

People are like sentences?

He pets our head and looks into the middle of the room, You know, he tries again, Relationships between people are similar to the relationships between ideas. People depend on one another for meaning.

We look at him until, a moment later, he waves his hand, Oh never mind, he laughs. That was a bit jejune, I guess.

We see that the man is ashamed, that he would like to impress us and we have not adequately validated the performance and that he wishes to take it back, to escape the embarrassing descent of his misstep. We feel tenderness for his shame, as if it were a meal we could share. We prize in that moment our mutual inability to be alone well, and for the tragedy of admitting it.

It's a nice thought, we say, and as he lifts the book back to his face, he pauses to look at us or through us and we think Now. Now, now.

At night we suffocate against his chest because he feels tender and to move would disrupt the feeling and so we breathe our own air in again, wondering how long we can stay like this before we will die. We remember that this is the goal, and so relax into the discomfort. To suffer is our penance for agreeing to live a little longer.

David talks about their vacations—beaches and ruins. Through him we learn what life could be like—desperately swimming from one raft of pleasure to the next. Each little island delaying the moment of drowning a little longer.

We think of his trips and bottles of Scotch and suits as fractions of the cost of our existence—one could pay a wintertime utility bill, another a quarter of our last year's taxes. We think of David's *keeping busy*. That motion is a distraction from pain. That the limitless search for abundance is a way to keep satisfaction at bay. That David runs to us so he will not have to confront the fragile shell of his own life, or the nothing it contains. That we do the same.

David cannot believe we don't travel. Have not taken an airplane. To where? We think of asking but say instead, Things being what they are, and he bristles for the first time. He believes we are being obstinate. It is the beginning of his disillusionment. What does that even mean? he asks. And because we know it will make him ashamed, and because his anger makes him look at us closely and without the mask of affection, we say we can't afford it. He sees the house again. The old things. He remembers we are not working and that he is generous. We do not bother to clarify: We can't afford to do things we don't want to do. We don't explain the siren's song of inertia. And even if he wants to save us, he knows he can't.

David says we are beautiful. David says we are smart. David says we are serious. David says we are too serious. David says to relax. David says we are a slut for his cock. David says we like that. David says we are a good little girl riding that cock. David says to look him in the eye, says he wants to see our pretty green eyes when he comes.

And if he doesn't say it, stops saying it, can no longer say it, it will cease to be true. Except the parts that we believe. The worst of it.

What was once a new language becomes a shared lexicon—first we are undressed by David and then he moves down our body until, mouth to cunt, we see only his gentle curls of graying hair. When we come against his mouth he climbs toward us, smiling and satisfied with himself, to slip inside of us and press the wet of us to our own mouth with his. We are later positioned over the edge of the bed, our hair is crossed in front of our throat and held tightly behind in David's fist like a rein. When he is ready to ejaculate he pulls away and we feel the soft spray of his come across our back and then his tongue as he licks it from our skin.

Each time David comes, the guilt shrinks so that the noose of shame which ties us together diminishes into habit. As the guilt diminishes so does the pleasure. And with the pleasure our worth. We adjust quickly to the ease of falling into bed, into each other, and question our fantasies, so easy now to fulfill, they are exhausting and real, so convenient that being filled with cock or wanted or choked or pressed into the mattress morphs smoothly into the familiar rhythm of a series of impassive words *comma* strokes *comma* another burst of fitful thrusts describing the body inside *period*

What is this word in the margin? David asks, holding up a book he's pulled from the shelf.

Gingivitis, we say, looking over his shoulder. He is in a white T-shirt and we believe for a moment this is a different time, and we are different people in a different life. That this is a story about an affair. It imbues the moment with possible tragedy and impossible romance. We are pained by his nearness.

He laughs. Why?

We shrug. It was a joke.

I don't get it.

Well, you laughed.

You're reading it again? David asks when he sees the book we are carrying to the couch.

Just skimming. He is quiet and studies us like a painting one does not particularly enjoy but finds curious. I thought you liked it? we say.

I do, I've just never felt that way, David says.

What way, we ask.

Blindly devoted. Longing at the expense of practicality. It's always gotten in the way of me rereading it to the end.

Oh? we say flatly. We aren't sure if this is intended to be an insult or if he lacks self-awareness.

Its real flaw, David announces, is that it purports to show all facets of the human experience but doesn't really. It doesn't have room for people who just want to do their work and go home and relax. I mean, there's laundry to be done. He looks back at the book in his hand. Contentment, he says finally. What ever happened to contentment?

I don't believe you're so content, we say. If you were, you wouldn't be here.

David says of the woman who left him before he married Lara: Not to be loved by the person you love does not mean you are unlovable.

We are moved by this vulnerable pronouncement. Then we suspect that Lara was his therapist. And that these are parting words.

We leave the house for the park for the shade of the trees for the distraction for the illusion of peace for the effect of its wall-lessness on our brain, as if our thoughts only go as far as the container our body is in. Every day as we stare at the ceiling above our bed we think disparaging thoughts about Lara—but here, we know better. She only appears small because we see her from a distance.

It is easy in the murmur of some natural space to predict our heartache and set it aside for later. We breathe long, full breaths of humid air.

We have grown accustomed to the sweater. We look for it when we return, and if we forget, we are pleased and startled by its presence. We rely on it to give the confusing pursuit of living continuity, to supply some external narrative that might provide the illusion of structure. Still, we are already steeling ourself for its predictable disappearance. We know already that this particular bend in the path will always remind us of it when it is gone. That we will not be able to enter the shade of the trees without anticipating its sudden red against the low stone wall and tangle of branches beyond. Without wondering what its new life is like. If he's happy.

David comes while we are away. We know because there is a note tucked between the screen and the frame. We hate and love that we have missed him. That he had occasion to miss us. That we had somewhere else to be.

We dream a giant woman carries us through space like a newborn confronted by the bewildering newness of everything. When we awaken alone in a pool of late summer sweat we long for this celestial mother—to climb upon her lap and weep, and will she stroke our hair? And will she coo comforting words? Will she love us? Will she say You are good, and which one of us will she mean? Which part of ourself, or the entirety of us? And will she hold our small feet in her enormous hands and, peddling them through the air, say: First this one, then this one, that's the way forward.

We dress quickly and leave without performing the rituals of the morning. Without coffee without brushing our teeth without standing in the middle of the house looking from side to side for something to seem worth doing.

We pass through the stone columns that announce the park's entrance. We cross a long field. We startle deer only a few steps away. We see wild strawberries but then wonder if they only look like strawberries. At the top of a hill we notice a trail veering off the path. We have passed this spot a dozen times this summer and never noticed it. We are impressed with our own lack of knowledge.

We follow the new path. It abuts a private property and we wonder if we will be scolded and prepare a speech to prove our innocence, but no one is there and no one says anything. We cross a small stream on a wooden board. We look between many pairs of trees for where the trail continues. We eventually choose to go vaguely left. Though only on the other side of the hill we usually climb, everything seems different. The earth more brown, the trees farther apart, the canopy more closed. We wander into a bramble of unripe blackberries. We think about ticks, about chiggers, about spiders, about the litany of our childhood fears, realizing only now that they all still exist. On the other side of the blackberries we come to a narrow road we don't recognize with no sidewalk. As we emerge, a car drives by and a young couple looks at us as if we are the wilderness.

We turn to go back the way we came. When we re-enter the pathless brown of newly fallen leaves we admit that we are lost, or rather, that we do not know where we are. There is pleasure in the discovery. We are not afraid because there is a road, which surely leads to civilization. Because we see the stream and know that eventually it will lead to the place we crossed it. Because though very large, the park is surrounded by homes and eventually, without the opportunity to starve or dehydrate, we will make it out alive. That it is entirely up to us to do so fills us with the thrill of independence. It occurs to us to want a love like this. Someone to get safely lost in. To be such a person.

David does not lie that he will leave his wife, but he lies that he has never felt this way: irresponsible, happy. And we do not ask him to leave her, but in the memories we make of the future he has no wedding band and he lives inside us, at the sink, at the foot of the bed, over the backs of chairs, and even when he is nowhere we can see—always behind always out of sight out of the corners of our eyes he is still in, moving in/through us like light traveling over porcelain figurines in glass-doored cabinets. David always the size of present tense, never moving toward or away, and when he appears on the front steps, green paint flaking, we open the door, and when he does not we wait, turn, wait, and stand on the cool cement, we imagine again that we are David, we look at us first through the eyes of the wealthy man, then as the man posed, absolutely still in our mind like the forever of ancient china plates resting perfectly in eternal patterns of dust.

He complains of Lara, of her monologue of criticism, of the more dishes he washes than she, of the toothpaste tube, and of nagging, and he says, I wonder how things would be different?

If what?

If we were together. He looks at us with a tenderness we mistrust.

We do not say Exactly the same. Us: dull and familiar. A wife. And someone else, easy, kept safely on the other side of town. We do not say there may be a reason for her bitterness and dissatisfaction. We do not say that it is the same reason we exist.

We pat him on the arm and nod, looking away and out the sheer lace of the curtain.

I wonder, we say finally.

Then one evening there is nothing to say.

There is something reassuring about watching closely as we are disabused of the illusion. Like having our eyes held open while the neighbor boy kicks a dog. Over and over. The willful hardening of the heart. The blood-rush of the power of staying still when we are asked to squirm.

We allow ourself instead the milquetoast superiority that comes with pity.

It is the end of the third week and already the rhythm of his visits/thrusts/days suggest that this/we, too, are ordinary. David says: New York. Or: cruise/theater/places people go (to buy things, to fill the empty spaces and hours, but we have no empty spaces in our mind for the crushing weight of people ready to buy or gamble or sit idle on a boat like immigrants waiting always for something good, pleading with a god for something better, then the unavoidable end and disappointment of returning to life, so each place far away will be remembered better than it was). In the easy domestic life/mounting lack of enthusiasm, David says, To the beach. And in our mind we see ourself standing on a hot soft yellow as he crashes into the white foam of waves. The blue-black of the mystery that waits below the surface. We shade our eyes from the harsh light of open sky with a pale hand, endless blue above and beyond in all directions, a collage of sand and scrubby trees from beach images accumulate behind us. We are an island to the sailor looking always for a place to land.

So easily David comes/goes and always the two are the same. Him in or outside, always just outside of our vision. Waiting, maybe for Lara to die with her mother, the whole life he promised disappearing easily to make room for Anything Else to move into its place, even the deep comfort of an understandable sadness, to replace the one that is so un-understandable to him or Lara. How could you not know it would be this way? We want to/don't say because who are we? We wonder even when David—made up entirely in our mind, maybe a ghost like everyone else in our life—is there, we wonder Who are we to ask this man why he stays? Or doesn't.

The fantasy is not to have David but to be known by David. That he will leave no stone unturned in his need to see more of us more deeply, that nothing he finds could diminish his desire. That even in our darkest recesses, we are acceptable, okay. That we will be okay. That, more than searching for an answer, he will be consumed by the curiosity to ask.

But David does not ask questions. David does not peer into the cavern of our heart. There is nothing he wants to know, and so he says without saying, we are not worth knowing.

Alone in the grocery store, we find David's ghost in front of bins of dried things and imagine the drops from the condensation of his milk dried into the floor, rehydrated and dried again. No place, we fear, will ever be real again without the memory of David baked into the skin of tiles and appliances and drinks and bars and shelves and each thing in each place, even new objects will be the idea of something David touched, the milk cartons in other towns representative of David's body, the most oblivious square of foreign, pale floor, the idea of all things, then always the idea of David.

We pick things from shelves wondering, hoping that David will be there, of course David is not there. David is at the office in our house in his house packing to be at the office/in our house and so our movements are not our own but the movements we see when we are David watching us. We place items in a red basket on our arm and evaluate our choices through David's eyes, through the eyes of money, through the eyes of the man David is when he is just himself, so that we cannot even remember the things we think about the choices we make. Cannot believe in our own mind, our mind so much the many points of David's view.

God is watching you, they said; and at night, when our legs ached, we cried for forgiveness for the sins God had watched all day, a voyeur. For touching ourself, for unkind thoughts, for boredom. It is easy to trust in the all-seeing power of those we worship. And when we touch ourself now, we do not pray for forgiveness; we pray that David is watching.

How does one throw off this persistent gaze? To live without needing a god is the original sin, the one that saved Eve from servitude. If only philosophically.

When we learn of Lara's imminent return, we agree to go to the beach with David. That a trip will be nice. That the weather is perfect for it, that the weather will soon change.

We sit quietly in his car for the first time since the first time, sliding over roads into parts of our city unseen for years. The road leads by a park of thick grass and strange sculptures where we were sent as a distraction from our own sudden arrival. The park, a diversion, now sprawls, spray-painted and bald. The road takes us past the church the grandparents drove to each week and we sat still and lifeless in itchy tights wondering when it would all be over and being reassured week after week—any day now. He will come any day.

We increase speed to enter the Shoreway to skip to the beaches of other towns and he doesn't say, Where I won't be recognized with a woman not my wife, he says, I've always been curious about— (another town falling into the cloudy water of the lake).

I've never been, either, we say, like it isn't a kind of goodbye.

Lara still far away, in our mind her mother taking a turn for the worse so that she must stay, we wade through hot mounds of sand, and it puffs like clouds between our toes. Our heels sink into the waves of burning powder and scratch against the cracked shells of pistachio-shaped clams; the sun rubs the bare skin of our back, calves, shoulders, and by the hand David leads us to the water's edge. We stop where brown water pulls up onto sand and flattens it into a cool, hard stoop from which to watch David as he runs childlike into the startling strength of tiny waves. He is laughing at the shock of the cold and the blue extends out from him in all directions. It is endless and terrifying, and when he calls to us and waves his arms, we smile from the water's edge, waving apathetically from the cool, hard sand.

The hot light echoes on the white foam that gathers around David's shoulders. What if he were a good man? Not what if he is, but what if he were a man who could be good for/with/to us? There is a sickening emptiness at the center of us. We burrow our feet into the sand and the pastor says, You can fill the void with the teachings of the Lord and righteousness, or you can allow the world to fill it for you, but it will fill. We ignore the pink shell of a tampon applicator a few feet away and force ourself to look out across the water, to try to see the land on the other side.

A strand of hair tickles our neck and we swat it away, the anxious certainty of our own inevitable ending so palpable that even our body feels as though it is creeping up on us. Now, we say, but it is lost in the hiss of the waves and wind and the abrasive call of seagulls. Now, now. The endless blue fills us with dread and we have never been so pathetic, have never confronted something so much larger than ourself.

He comes back dripping and wiping silty water from his face. Come in, he says, pulling our hand.

Not yet. We shrug.

Not yet! He laughs at us—absurd, hot, our skin turning a tender shade of pink already. But it feels so good, he says, and loops a cool, wet arm around our waist and leads us in as our skin pricks in the oily water.

I don't know where I'm going, we admit.

He says absently, You're fine.

We try to protest but it comes out foolishly.

David turns, tucks the hair blowing around our face behind an ear. What's wrong?

I don't know how to swim, we say, and shrug. It's true enough to stand in for an explanation of our fear.

Why didn't you tell me? he asks tenderly, and we shrug again.

The water laps our thighs and we sway in the current as things we cannot see move against us in the water. We gaze beyond him to the beach, solid, baking in the sun. There is something seductive about the terrifying depths. The possibility that there is nothing we could do to save ourself. That a lake may as well be an ocean, that there would be no use in struggling.

Try floating on your back, David suggests, holding us tight against him, dragging us farther from shore. He relaxes his hold, leaving a hand at our back to help us perform the trick of suspending our body like a corpse on the surface of the water, his other hand behind our head. Keep breathing, he says, and we do as he says. An arm slithers under our legs and we shiver. We move like a bottle out to sea, David all the while getting shorter, closer until we float by his shoulders and he leans to kiss our mouth. You're fine, he says to our lips. His voice fills and drains from the kiddie pool of our ears, a hand slides over our stomach and cups water to pour over our thighs.

How are you? he asks.

Fine, we repeat, a mechanism of fear, cleaning the words of our own mind with his, but our breaths come in short bursts and we involuntarily bite our lips together when we think a wave might pull us under.

We see nothing but the pale blue of sky and his face in shadow as we bob on each small crest of water. He turns to look up and down the beach and we do not lift our head, do not strain to sit on the water, as if it would grow firm under us as under the feet of Christ, though we are hungry just to see the beach still secure against the horizon. Ye of so little faith, He says.

There's no one out here, he says with disappointment, as if the empty beach were a commentary on our decision to come.

So if we die, no one will even know. We try to joke but are comforted by how much we mean it.

David laughs, I had no idea you would be so afraid. And again: Why didn't you tell me?

It's hard to imagine how terrifying things are before you're in them, we say flatly.

David fingers the cloth at the crotch of our suit, pulling it aside to thumb the pink of us. Relax, he coaches, a hand at the small of our back to help us stay afloat, fingers spread in the faint pattern of a shower on our back. I won't let anything hurt you.

We know he is promising things outside of his control, and he bends to lick the flesh he's exposed.

The water at the corners of our eyes burns salty, our

own. We bite our tongue until it tastes metallic like an old spoon, like the teeth marks inside our lips after sucking David; we don't insist that it is because of him that we will be hurt. His tongue falters and we imagine he will drown and leave us or he is fine and will let us drown or we will both live but the delicate flesh of our cunt will burn in the sun/the filthy ecosystems of the lake will seep into us and poison us slowly.

David replaces the fabric and with some magic floats next to us, smiling to himself, reaches out and touches us lightly as we struggle to breathe.

The uncomfortable pull of our burnt skin against the sticky leather of the car's seat is a nagging reminder that we have done something wrong, to the woman to ourself to the women rotting in boxes who would say we should know better and their voices, and the voice of David of all the Davids so loud we cannot hear our own or begin to imagine what it might say. There is a vague but growing malcontent that makes us feel petulant. The trees burst by in streaks of dead branches and green life and David changes the radio station. We notice the minutia of his existence, the dark hairs on his wrists and way he holds the steering wheel at ten and two like a student.

We are silent as we drive through small towns toward the interstate but once, as we gain speed as if escaping the day and the performance of being together, he touches our thigh briefly, the fingertips brushing sensitive skin with caution, we look from the contrast of his tan skin against our pink to his face, the brow furrowed with fleeting evidence of concern and replaced quickly by the trail of his lips tightening into a resigned smile.

Though the fear of missing him fills us with a silent alarm, we leave the house. We take a circuitous route past the cemetery to get to the park, and through the park to the woods, and once in the woods down a road that leads past hidden maintenance buildings and tunnels with graffiti. It is a place easy to be afraid, and this is what gives us hope that something beautiful and untouched lies on the other side.

A glittering mass in the path ahead lures us. The undulating waves of reflected light make the object seem out of focus. We come close and stare at it for many long moments. Like the hazy dizziness of standing too quickly, our brain struggles to make meaning of what we're seeing. Then we see teeth. And the stretched holes that once held eyes but now release a cascade of larvae, like a waterfall of individual tears. The white, writhing bodies spill infinitely from every hole in the rodent's small carcass. We are repulsed and think of our own corpse—found one day in the house, months decomposed—that this is not how we would like to be found. But almost immediately we think that this is how we want to live. So full of life that it spills from every orifice. And for the first time we understand our grandparents' blind pursuit of the Holy Spirit, a longing to be inhabited and consumed by it. We think it must look like this.

We know that Lara has returned when David does not appear in the evening or the one after. The terrible flood of the obvious replaces the logic of waiting. It is said that man cannot know the day or the hour of the return, but we do.

The days come long and distinct, ticking by in clean hours recreated by hash marks on skin, no trails of blood, just the white ash of a fingernail against an arm, leg, the pink trail of the growing nails scraped across the meat of a shoulder. And like the superficial scrapes, each hour disappears into the next and always the next hour comes empty and defined, marked by the thunderous tick of a clock, as if always we rest with our ear to a timepiece.

On the fourth day, David is on the cement step, a button missing on his shirt, and it opens into a cave so we immediately wonder who he has become in those long hours while we hoped/waited, scolded ourself not to hope/wait. He is disheveled, knocks and enters quickly; in a few weeks he believes he belongs and he enters and we are standing by the table and he comes to us his shirt open distractingly where the button is missing and we see the chest we have looked at so many times naked, but half-hidden we feel we are stealing glances and he says with none of the shyness of his first visit that Lara is back and he's been busy (and we have stopped being the other but the thing, a regular life hard to maintain, we should be something easy. A thing that needs nothing. But we are instead old, requiring maintenance, and do not solve the problems of loneliness and are so much more difficult for being hidden, unacceptable). And as we fall from waking dream to the sad, yellow light of our life, we watch David fall reluctantly from lust into the reedy panic of regret, guilt rubbed out by our hand on his cock and reawakened by Lara's appearance in their home. Home the thing they make in the clean, white walls of their easy but empty lives, and she needs so much to be comforted now, after her exhausting trip. So cruel of her family to wait to start dying until she is so accustomed to them being there. But for David the excitement of the other, of us, must be fading already into a question of practicality, a calculated value of the affair, of us, like a tab, a too-low return on investment.

David says he has not talked about Lara for our sake, what might happen when she returns, how much she needs him. And we don't ask, Whose life has been made easier by the convenient absence of Lara?

David does not stay the night—cannot stay more than a moment—but wants to know How are you? And we know that he does not want to know how we are, about the constant weight around our neck that feels like sleep, he wants only to find some new place to leave a part of the burden of being himself and so we say Fine. We are fine. And we guide the man to the couch and we rub first the graying hairline and the lines around the eyes and mouth and the man closes his eyes and we rub the pale fabric of his dress shirt, our fingers slip in the gap where we see the chest hairs and touch them with our fingers, long and straight hairs, a nest, we think: But—

and: I love you—

and take it back immediately.

We kneel before the man and undress him, so familiar the weight and movement of his hips as he lifts them to let us, his absence of expression expressing the folds of feeling he is carrying in his stomach like a briefcase. We kiss the hairy flesh around the soft cock and there is a flicker, and we knead the muscles of the man's thighs and David pets slowly our head, and we take the cock, still only half-hard, into our mouth, and David relaxes into an extension of the couch, a pillow where we rest our head, only to lift and lower again to rest, and he furrows his brow, trying to concentrate, but he is with Lara, a sound comes from his throat like weeping but his jaw clenches. He pulls our hair and presses us down onto the cock and we follow the strained lifting of his hips and when finally he is done, we are done, and he is crying the notcrying of a man. He fastens his pants, ashamed, and kisses our mouth full of his come and, standing, pulls us to standing and holds us for a moment very tightly, the come still the loose wet muscle of an oyster in the shell of our mouth.

David says I have to go./(Lara.)/I'll see you soon./I'll see you.

The sun bakes first the rain from the streets then roof then moisture trapped in the grain of every chair wall floor bedpost dries to the dusty lightness we remember. The house recovers the desert, its bones the same powder white of the bones recorded to our ears, cracks and fissures easy to see and held tenderly inside its imperfect shell. David is mysterious, absent, and in the empty spaces we find more empty spaces—each place the place he has or hasn't touched. Did all the generations of us feel the absence of David? Was that what drove the great-grandparents from their farm into town, and grandparents to church, and the parents to their unforgivable behavior and to our own adolescent longing that pinned our weak body to the floor with a weight like too much gravity. The sluggishness now in our bones like the lethargic movements of youth. Useless mix of restraint and bursting inside ourself against the itchy carpet of the bedroom until a light knock and the soft voices of our mother's parents. And so in this new sort of weakness we are the dust storm moving nothing; dust shining in batons of light dry our throat, and we sit in the unnatural glow of a single light bulb like a spotlight for a performance we have not rehearsed.

In the mirror above the bathroom sink, haloed in yellowing bottles of lotion, bubble bath, powders long discontinued, we see though we sleep fitfully through the night that there is no rest. Lines of worry furrow our brow and the pain inside our head/breasts/pit of the stomach create a new cloud across our face—the face the only thing in the house that ever changes, we consider the difference: the more or less we never always want to cry or eat or sleep and we wonder about these tides as they move through the house, through us. They are the cobwebby movements of slippered feet against old floor hovering above darkness within darkness.

In the night we stare at the ceiling, believing in everything that has crashed against the sand of our home. To leave. What leaves us? Who belonged to us so that they could leave us anyway? What tired stories had we believed so that we'd thought the house: ours, and the man: ours, and the growing discomfort in our body and the weather and glint in the sun: ours? In the quiet and hum of electricity, David is in everything, is now the much larger nothing in the house like the grandparents dead, and parents finally dead, and great-grandparents gone, and as they all decompose in their vaults, the dried bugs and embroidered napkins and evangelical pamphlets in their final resting place under armchairs and in the corners of bookshelves and quietly growing powdered like bones.

We trip through the house in bare feet, a moth in a shoebox, midafternoon sun poking holes in the windows like a cardboard lid, and the world has lost finally its luster. We are full and empty and terrified and like jerking awake just before sleep, the steep slope always ready give way as we fall, we are ready to die when our swollen breasts imagine David, sucking, and we think of the gray and brown hairs as we stroke his head in our mind, the head to breast, and finally, we miss him.

We are amazed by his distance, as if he's recovered from us like the momentary hallucinations of a fever. But where does the fever go when it stops shaking the lungs? Where do we go now?

In the woods, a woman jogs by. Pets are on leashes. Men stand with fishing poles. The world becomes a cast of characters with accessories to prove their belonging. Only we seem aimless and empty-handed. As we amble along the path we forgive the smokers their cigarettes and the old women their perfume. We forgive the dog-walkers who leave feces in their wake that will work its way into the intricate patterns on the soles of shoes. We forgive David his carelessness. We forgive Lara her existence, her mother her recovery. We believe that we, too, will recover. We believe in some sort of future. We choose a bewildered optimism because, if nothing else, it smacks of pragmatism, and practicality, if unremarkable, still seems respectable.

We round the bend and the sweater is gone.

The emptiness that has gnawed at us all week takes on a crippling permanence. There is no way to reach out. There is no number to call. There is no one waiting for us.

We ask its ghost: Is there something else on the other side of misery—another body to wrap yourself around?

When we give in to the gravity of our irreparable situation and the monotonous drone of our malcontent, we return to the floor of the living room. We stare at the dusty plaster we watched over David's shoulder and think of the doctor and her sure voice, the words stretched tight by the waves of pain in our head and the sluggish, milky consciousness that has replaced the sharp edges of our longing. The reflection off all our glittering trash has lost its golden hue and shines instead with the awful fierceness of sun on a used-car lot: a million windshields, a skyscraper, the white glare of summer on endless water, the ocean, the lake, a million of someone else's childhood creeks all gold sun, white in dizzying reflection. The stained tile, David's stained tile, always his even before he was born when the great-grandparents first laid the tile for him to stand on, waiting generations to soak up the blood-red of wine, the house dying now around this wound.

We sit or pace or stand idly, an animal, a vulture, waiting, maybe always waiting, to understand the senseless trajectory of the past and its evidence.

We pick things up, move them as David might, and are struck by the rings of dust and faded colors of paint left in their place, and we follow the trail of these things, the dolls we never touched pulled from a shelf, better hidden in a drawer still full of cone-shaped brassieres, wide elastic flaking into blond curls of dolls falling out of their plastic heads when touched or bumped shut into the drawer. Vases not filled with roses from the garden not maintained and lace made and draped carefully and records and cassettes and radios broken like arms, their electrical cords thin, brown veins waiting to catch fire from two weak prongs trailing behind green fake leather recliner, plastic and cracked, and jam jars printed cartoon or floral and the thick jelly of bath soap. We carry all of these things below to the cool emptiness of basement, the fearful place becoming a shelter from the sweltering indifference of the house. All things like

David wade further from our shore, and we abandon them there in puddles that have formed from rain in the corners. Everything blue-black like a bruise. We fill the model of the house with the house's belongings, bulletins on wildlife preservation and a Christmas church service, we abandon table runners and phone books, pans and pots fill with dog figurines, old tools, and cologne. Old mattresses and wood stove and hammer and saw and curious stringed instrument and typewriters and filing boxes and photographs and men's boots. All of these things disguise themselves in the basement as David—as nothing.

For the first time since the last funeral, we open the door to the grandparents' room. It smells more of them than even the house. Roses and wood and dust. A time capsule of an ordinary life that no longer exists.

And then, as we kneel to pull three matching pairs of overalls in our grandfather's size from the back of the bottom drawer of our grandparents' dresser, we find a shoebox rattling with trinkets. We recognize instantly a tinted lip balm given to us by a friend in fourth grade. The sparkle and flavor had been intoxicating. It made us feel beautiful, real, important, and for this it was confiscated. A school photo of ourself at twelve years old, two horns painted around our head in white-out. The suggestion of Satan so transgressive, the self-destruction so powerful a feeling. It had been found under our pillow and went where all the things we loved went—to this box in their bureau. The skeleton keychain with jeweled eyes, a picture of a gun torn from a magazine, a stolen blood-red nail polish, a chain with the gold partly rubbed off, a crucified Jesus hanging grotesquely by a jump ring in the chain. A graven image. We touched them all with the reverence of religious relics, evidence of our former selfhood, and all of these things mixed with other artifacts we didn't remember: a bottle of perfume the size of our thumb, a beaded bracelet with half a heart with the letters BF burned into the wooden charm, a deck of cards—an invitation to gamble—a palm-sized spiral notebook with the word Private written on the front in childish scrawl, on the inside the name Ruth.

We can't help but confuse these objects with the physical person of our mother. The perfume smells like alcohol and rotten cherries, and we breathe it so deeply we feel faint and then nauseous and crawl to a waste can by the door to retch. We sit with our back against the doorframe, catching our breath, the phantom smell of the perfume still lingering in our nostrils with the very real smell of our vomit. We hold our breath to replace the cap of the perfume and slide the too-tight bracelet over our hand, letting the beads pinch the skin of our wrists. As we sit on the bed, a fine mist of dust scatters. We flip through the pages of our mother's private notebook, both desperate for a secret message and embarrassed for invading her childhood privacy.

On the second page, each line is filled with the same message in careful but unbeautiful script:

I love Bobby.

We look through every drawer and recess and box with renewed vigor, but the only objects that remain of our mother, or the person she was, are those few mementos of her as a failure in the eyes of the grandparents. Perhaps, we think, there are no better artifacts. No better secret code than our shared space in their gallery of sin. We'd never felt so close to her, or to ourself.

We stop removing everything when there is nothing left to remind us of anything; the voices are for the moment at a loss for words, everything is choked, and in the house's new barrenness we stand above the replica of the house, feeling its haunting presence below us, its gold-flecked floors made of the house's gold-flecked floors, flesh of my flesh, we move through the rooms and die in each one. We stuff the small spaces with ancient newspaper and mousetraps. We destroy the world the grandparents made like an angry god, and in the end we rest with an exhaustion that suffices for satisfaction, still smelling the oppressively sweet scent of spoiled cherries.

We sit on the couch at the far end of the house and look down its empty expanse. We don't understand who we are becoming or if it will be better than who we were before, but we know that we are angry, and that the anger is our own.

We wonder about Bobby. Was it Bobby who drove her to a life of sin? Her first inkling of something different, something tantalizing because it was forbidden. For this we love Bobby, too. And we whisper it aloud into the emptiness.

I love Bobby.

I love Bobby.

I love Bobby.

The house is skeletal around us, foreign and vacant. In the strange space, we are unsure who we are—did we ever know? The mother, grandmother, did they know? Does anyone know how to live?

We are full with grief and grasping and want to empty ourself/life/the house. To remove the trash left by the years, to be gutted, to be made clean.

The alignment of heavenly bodies paints a rainbow across the chipping walls and over a portrait of the desert, and as in our youth we feel a magnetic pull. God sent a rainbow, says the grandmother, as a sign of His eternal love.

We know that the colors are the result of the mechanics of light and a tchotchke purchased in a gift shop and hung in a window, forgotten by our frantic dismantling, and that it has only just now caught the distant sun in its glass. But we know that that is no small feat, either.

We hold out our hand so the rainbow is cupped in our palm and the magic of the light travels across our skin. We are surprised by its concentrated heat, and the warmth of desire flickers, and we remember an early longing, older than David or God. A whisper of a memory from a life before the grandparents and a more distant house activated by the projection of light, a memory so detached from space that it is all impression: the feeling of wonder.

We dream the house in lightning, an X-ray: still-life black and white of the electric snap casts the shadow of everything now hidden back into the dark, dustless holes they used to fill. And in the dream nothing is not absence, but all of the somethings between the things we pick up, move, remove, and like this we move through David's nothing, the thick air of him left between all the things taken away.

In the morning we snap the too-tight elastic of our mother's beaded bracelet against our wrist. We sit at the edge of the bed, meditating on the sting. We think of her, forty years before. How miserable she must have been.

The days without David pass in cruel slowness. We are led through space by a leash of heartache. A week feels like a month of the screen door swinging Come, Go, but no body comes/goes. Our selfishness is the shapeless hallway of the yellow house where we mop the dry cracks in the floor with our tears and shine the wooden back of chairs with the running we wipe from our nose. We pray our silent love to Bobby. We try to become the woman who got away, whatever the price.

But who are we in any other context? The fear that David is a counterfeit—that he is empty, that he is less real than we'd hoped, that he is some human machine—pales in comparison to the fear that we are the fraud. That we lack adequate kindness or intelligence to be a sufficient person, that our lack of physical struggles have made us lazy, that crying over our own relative ease is just another ploy to make us feel better about it and to spare us the effort of thinking of others.

It has nothing to do with wanting to die and everything to do with our inadequacy at living.

As we cry into our bathwater, we become sensitive to a different sort of suffering: every moment is ripe with opportunity for transcendent pain. Alone in the tub with electric appliances tantalizingly close, we are struck by a dread much bigger than our own—that it is not just the man who dies at the end of the book, but everyone. People are vanishing, forgotten and alone in bathtubs all over the world. Who will find them? Who will hold them as they cross over? We press on our sternum to keep our heart from leaking out of our chest. We are crushed by cosmic grief caused by our inadequacy to traverse the gaping maw of human indifference. Everything is lost. The trees that sway in the backyard. The families in the park. Our parents. The abandoned sweater. There is nothing we can do, but the Sisyphean impulse is there to push against it senselessly.

This new ambivalence toward death has a parasite of sickening hopefulness.

The smell of a neighbor's dinner wafts through an open window. Broccoli, maybe. There are people just next door making their way through over-cooked vegetables. Everyone, we believe now, is suffering. We are all so sad, and who will know? Who will come be lonely with us?

We try to multiply the number of days we might have left on earth to see if we could spend a day with each person with whom we share this spinning rock, just to keep them company—us company—if only for a moment. We will be the ambassador of suffering to the whole world.

We will do nothing, we know, because loneliness is a disease that other people can't cure. Even so, there has grown inside of us the need to watch the end as it approaches of its own accord. To suffer more fully. To meet death as we once met David: offering ourself so there is nothing it can/t take.

We know the reward for this courage will not be ease, but the promise of some new plight.

We wake with the confusion of waking in a foreign place, but it is only the absence of everything we've ever known that causes this sensation. In that brief moment, as we try to remember who and where we are, we forget David and our sadness.

When the memory returns, we look at it like a rude guest. An uninvited visitor of whom we have grown tired.

Our hand is taut and red and stiff without circulation from the tight bracelet. We take it off and tuck it under the pillow. For a moment we worry for its safety there, but remember the grandparents won't find it.

On the ninth day, David stands on the front step and says Regret and Stronger Will and Fidelity. We imagine these words rubbed into his chest like an old jar of vapors by Lara's fingers because she knows: All they needed, really needed, was to talk. We stand in our new body seeing with new eyes but also with David's eyes with the unforgiving eyes of another life easier, better, without us. We see with Lara's eyes and those of our grandmother and great-grandmother before so that nothing becomes the place—not where David has stood—but where he stands on the peeling step and he doesn't say Goodbye or I'll miss you or any words that would mean he'd ever been here at all. His presence is the only admission of guilt. Already gone in this way, he says all the words that mean Lara, or mean that we have always been alone, we would be unreasonable to ask for more, we must have known this would happen, and he knows, Lara says in his mouth Commitment and New Start, and maybe in our silence there appears a moment for admission but instead comes out: I'm sorry if you—

He will never say: *Sorry I.* Just: You/What did you do to make me sorry? He says between the other words that can never be discerned from the piles of trash that make us up.

We dress our mind in our old body so we can remember it is easy not to cry, not to want the man; we squint instead into the sun as it lowers behind David earlier than ever before, before anything we can remember. We whisper in our mind *I love Bobby* over and over so as not to hear what David is saying. Everything is all blue sky shooting out from him, the white trail of a plane leading to nothing—but then we imagine the head at our breast, we shade our eyes with our hand, the hand we use to wipe crying snot from our face. We say, Oh.

The cold filling our throat, the smile is poison on our mouth. It is easy enough to say: I understand. And we watch ourself act out ourself, and we need only to say so little before we can collapse back into the still, hot house.

I'm happy things are working out for you, we say.

He is Relieved and Surprised, but there is the unspoken: Hurt. Wanting only to have meant more to us than we to him. We close the distance between us. Resting fingertips on his arm, we kiss his cheek he neither offers nor refuses. We step back into the dark hallway and, as if caught by a shadow or the right reflection of light off some dull, white surface, we are lit up. David, maybe for the first time, recognizes that there is a change and terrified asks with sudden, honest concern: Are you okay?

We smile with warmth manufactured: I'm fine.

He is not assuaged and asks to come in and, though we hate it/long for it/hate that we long for it, we open the door, a sickness coating our lungs as he passes. In the kitchen we see through his eyes the missing everything. The empty walls and counters and tables. What happened? he asks, and maybe he does not remember why he is here now, to leave us and this place where we fuck where he has come to say: not fuck—but now, maybe a new place and us: maybe new, and he: the same, more the same than before as he struggles to match himself to some man he was or was supposed to be.

Cleaning, we offer lightly.

But your family's stuff— As if crushed by the weight of absence, the absence we've felt since he stood, as he stands now, carefully balancing at the edge of the counter. The same sadness he feels for the man who will die. And he cannot believe that what happens to the man in the story is happening to him. That life could move on without him.

Everything must go, we say dully, and we are still pretending like children to be man and woman, and we pretend to be Fine, a good woman, Fine. David says, in the endless blue of the lake, You are fine, and we are his to do with whatever, to throw away or hide in cupboards and to be Fine. And it is clear in this house, that we are living and burrowed into ourself, and that David is the sand the oyster rejects and even inside us, the house our body makes, rejects him.

Are you leaving? he asks, and maybe the Resolve in front of the house becomes more complicated when it is no longer his, no longer Lara's, but ours, ours to take from him, our fantasy the man who comes and stays the night and in the morning kisses the cunt and then the forehead and then to work, and it is ours to take. Ours to ask for nothing, and to give nothing, to accept no generosity, to be nothing. We see him not as the cause of our sadness but a vessel for it, an explanation, and his departure marks only an inconvenient shifting to a new problem: ourself.

Maybe, we say, knowing immediately that it is true, never having considered it until this moment. And David feels the trap of his life he will return to and leave and be forced again to return to: he knows himself now and that while we die from him, leave for a faraway emptiness of our own making, he has no new self to inhabit. He sees as we see the house, barren except for the stain he's left, and sad/empty/gone from everything, he says again:

Are you okay?

I'm fine *period* Our smile becomes heavy and he wraps us in arms and kisses our forehead and says only, at least, I'm sorry.

Easy, now: I'm sorry. When there is nothing he can do and he knows we are not his to do for, and more importantly that we will not ask. We know the weight of nothing that will follow as he tries to make up for himself. Now. Now, now.

Our hands move familiar over the clean, bright body, and his fingers find our hair and the easy remembered pull and our head back he kisses our mouth we rest tender breasts against him, his thumb slides over nipple and near pain we press against him and he walks us backward to the sink, presses, lifts our grandmother's thin dress up to our waist. A finger sliding in as if searching for what he has left and our breath in his ear and he pulls away to turn us around, to push us over the sink before he can think his way out of it, the sunlight on the faucet distant through the milkglass of our watery vision, and we will the tears not to fall down our face, the dress pushed up and the man sliding cock against wet and then the first slap, and the second, and we falter, grab for the edge of the sink, particles of food dried to the pale peach basin, the faucet's decade of slow drips make a thin green-brown mineral trail to the drain. The sink's lip pressing into our ribs, the flesh below our breasts, and we think Tits and pretend that this is all that has happened, sex. It was nothing, we say to ourself as we hear the next crack of a slap before we feel it. The faucet glimmers a dead bird and the come lands across our back like a flock.

His cock presses against the flesh of our ass as he rubs the come in, puts his hand to our face to taste, to eat his body, to make his body our body again. He rests his head on our shoulder, bites gently, holds us before moving away to pull together his pants. We stay, staring into the sink, dripping wet onto the floor.

We'd seen him as the answer to the infinite list of our problems. To the problem of being. But he has become a new problem without a solution. Or with an obvious solution, yielding only new problems.

David sits, rolling on a wheeled chair through his own empty space. We wipe our face with our hands before stepping out of the sticky underclothes and crossing the narrow room to lean against the counter beside him. We consider the lack of emotion we feel at his turned head. He wheels nearer to us with awkward minced steps. It's incongruous with the seriousness of the moment and we want to laugh. He wraps his arms around our thighs and rests his forehead against the small bulge of our stomach, just below our navel.

He is silent and maybe now there is also Resentment, for taking first his good intentions and then his fantasy away, for reminding him of it and denying him. We are at fault that he must return to the good woman, good wife who loves him.

We stay like this until the bitterness and sadness and loneliness and many adjectives of our affair settle into the boredom of waiting for it to pass and for David to leave—his body growing smaller the farther it is from us, haloed in the glint of the horizon beyond him, the allure of places just past what we can see—and for the next thing to arrive.

TATIANA RYCKMAN is the author of the novel *The Ancestry of Objects* (Deep Vellum Publishing), and the novella *I Don't Think of You (Until I Do)* (Future Tense), as well as three chapbooks of prose. She is the editor of Awst Press and has been an artist in residence at Yaddo, Arthub, and 100W Corsicana. Her work has appeared in *Tin House*, *Lithub*, *Paper Darts*, *Barrelhouse*, and other publications. Tatiana can be found on airplanes or at tatianaryckman.com.

Thank you all
for your support.
We do this for you,
and could not do
it without you.

PARTNERS

FIRST EDITION MEMBERSHIP
Anonymous (9)
Donna Wilhelm

TRANSLATOR'S CIRCLE
Ben & Sharon Fountain
Cullen Schaar and Amanda Alvarez
Jeff Lierly
Meriwether Evans

PRINTER'S PRESS MEMBERSHIP
Allred Capital Management
Charles Dee Mitchell
David Tomlinson & Kathryn Berry
Farley Houston
Jeff Leuschel
John Rodgers
Judy Pollock
Loretta Siciliano
Lori Feathers
Mark Perkins
Mary Ann Thompson-Frenk & Joshua Frenk
Matthew Rittmayer
Nick Storch
Pixel and Texel
Robert Appel
Social Venture Partners Dallas
Stephen Bullock
Thomas DiPiero

AUTHOR'S LEAGUE
Christie Tull
David Hale Smith
Jacob Seifring
Lissa Dunlay
Orin Snyder
Stephen Bullock

PUBLISHER'S LEAGUE
Adam Rekerdres
Justin Childress
Kay Cattarulla
KMGMT
Olga Kislova
Peggy Carr
Susan B. Reese

EDITOR'S LEAGUE
Ali Haider
Amrit Dhir
Brandon Kennedy
Chris Pan
Dallas Sonnier
Garth Hallberg
Greg McConeghy
Jeremy Hays and Cody Cosmic
Joe Milazzo
Joel Garza
Kate & Art Anderson
Linda Nell Evans
L. Robert Stevens
Mary Moore Grimaldi
Maryam O. Baig
Michael Mullins
Mike Kaminsky
Mya Coursey
Nancy Rebal
P&C Sandoval
Patricia Storace
Ron Restrepo
Ryan Todd
Scott & Katy Nimmons
Sean Cotter
Stephanie Keller
Stephen Goldfarb
Steven Harding
Suejean Kim
Susan and Warren Ernst
Symphonic Source
Tim Coursey
Wendy Belcher

READER'S LEAGUE
Bianca Rochell
Caitlin Baker
Cameron E Greene
Caroline Casey
Carolyn Mulligan
Chilton Thomson
Cole Suttle
Corine Fox
Edward Fox
Elena Westbrook
Evelyn Fox
Gavin Newman
Jeff Waxman
Jerry Hawkins
Jorge Marcos
JR. Forasteros
Kate Johnson
Kayla Finstein
Kelly Britson
Kelly & Corby Baxter
Linda Mowl
Lisa and Donovan Davidson
Maria Coward
Marian Schwartz & Reid Minot
Marlo D. Cruz Pagan
Mary Dibbern
Matthew Pitt
Meghan Lapham
Russ Mullins
Sue Owens
Thomas Lee
Tina Lin
Tony Messenger
Valerie Cooper

DEEP ELLUM CIRCLE
Alan Shockley
Amanda & Bjorn Beer
Andrew Yorke
Anonymous (10)
Ashley Milne Shadoin
Bob & Katherine Penn
Brandon Childress
Charley Mitcherson
Charley Rejsek
Cheryl Thompson
Chloe Pak
Cone Johnson
CS Maynard
Daniel J. Hale

Walmart

pixel texel

ADDITIONAL DONORS, CONT'D

Daniela Hurezanu
Danielle Dubrow
Denae Richards
Dori Boone-Costantino
Ed Nawotka
Elizabeth Gillette
Elizabeth Van Vleck
Erin Kubatzky
Ester & Matt Harrison
Grace Kenney
Hillary Richards
JJ Italiano
Jeremy Hughes
John Darnielle
Jonathan Legg
Julie Janicke Muhsmann
Kelly Falconer
Kevin Richardson
Laura Thomson
Lea Courington
Lee Haber
Leigh Ann Pike
Lowell Frye
Maaza Mengiste
Mark Haber
Mary Cline
Max Richie
Maynard Thomson
Michael Reklis
Mike Soto
Mokhtar Ramadan
Nikki & Dennis Gibson
Patrick Kukucka
Patrick Kutcher
Rev. Elizabeth & Neil Moseley
Richard Meyer
Sam Simon
Sherry Perry
Skander Halim
Sydneyann Binion
Stephen Harding
Stephen Williamson
Susan Carp
Theater Jones
Tim Perttula
Tony Thomson

SUBSCRIBERS

Audrey Golosky
Ben Fountain
Ben Nichols
Carol Trimmer
Caroline West
Charles Dee Mitchell
Charlie Wilcox
Chris Mullikin
Chris Sweet
Courtney Sheedy
Dan Pope
Daniel Kushner
Derek Maine
Elisabeth Cook
Fred Griffin
Heath Dollar
Hillary Richards
Ian Robinson
Jason Linden
Jody Sims
Joe Milazzo
John Winkelman
Kate Ivey
Kenneth McClain
Kirsten Hanson
Lance Stack
Lisa Balabanlilar
Luke Bassett
Margaret Terwey
Martha Gifford
Megan Coker
Michael Binkley
Michael Elliott
Michael Lighty
Molly Lunn
Nathan Dize
Neal Chuang
Radhika Sharma
Shelby Vincent
Stephanie Barr
Ted Goff
Vincent Granata
William Pate

AVAILABLE NOW FROM DEEP VELLUM

MICHÈLE AUDIN · *One Hundred Twenty-One Days*
translated by Christiana Hills · FRANCE

BAE SUAH · *Recitation*
translated by Deborah Smith · SOUTH KOREA

EDUARDO BERTI · *The Imagined Land*
translated by Charlotte Coombe · ARGENTINA

CARMEN BOULLOSA · *Texas: The Great Theft* · *Before* · *Heavens on Earth*
translated by Samantha Schnee · Peter Bush · Shelby Vincent · MEXICO

LEILA S. CHUDORI · *Home*
translated by John H. McGlynn · INDONESIA

SARAH CLEAVE, ed. · *Banthology: Stories from Banned Nations* ·
IRAN, IRAQ, LIBYA, SOMALIA, SUDAN, SYRIA & YEMEN

ANANDA DEVI · *Eve Out of Her Ruins*
translated by Jeffrey Zuckerman · MAURITIUS

ALISA GANIEVA · *Bride and Groom* · *The Mountain and the Wall*
translated by Carol Apollonio · RUSSIA

ANNE GARRÉTA · *Sphinx* · *Not One Day*
translated by Emma Ramadan · FRANCE

JÓN GNARR · *The Indian* · *The Pirate* · *The Outlaw*
translated by Lytton Smith · ICELAND

GOETHE · *The Golden Goblet: Selected Poems*
translated by Zsuzsanna Ozsváth and Frederick Turner · GERMANY

NOEMI JAFFE · *What Are the Blind Men Dreaming?*
translated by Julia Sanches & Ellen Elias-Bursac · BRAZIL

CLAUDIA SALAZAR JIMÉNEZ · *Blood of the Dawn*
translated by Elizabeth Bryer · PERU

JUNG YOUNG MOON · *Seven Samurai Swept Away in a River* · *Vaseline Buddha*
translated by Yewon Jung · SOUTH KOREA

FOWZIA KARIMI · *Above Us the Milky Way: An Illuminated Alphabet* · USA

KIM YIDEUM · *Blood Sisters*
translated by Ji yoon Lee · SOUTH KOREA

JOSEFINE KLOUGART · *Of Darkness*
translated by Martin Aitken · DENMARK

YANICK LAHENS · *Moonbath*
translated by Emily Gogolak · HAITI

FOUAD LAROUI · *The Curious Case of Dassoukine's Trousers*
translated by Emma Ramadan · MOROCCO

MARIA GABRIELA LLANSOL · *The Geography of Rebels Trilogy: The Book of Communities; The Remaining Life; In the House of July & August*
translated by Audrey Young · PORTUGAL

PABLO MARTÍN SÁNCHEZ · *The Anarchist Who Shared My Name*
translated by Jeff Diteman · SPAIN

DOROTA MASŁOWSKA · *Honey, I Killed the Cats*
translated by Benjamin Paloff · POLAND

BRICE MATTHIEUSSENT · *Revenge of the Translator*
translated by Emma Ramadan · FRANCE

LINA MERUANE · *Seeing Red*
translated by Megan McDowell · CHILE

VALÉRIE MRÉJEN · *Black Forest*
translated by Katie Shireen Assef · FRANCE

FISTON MWANZA MUJILA · *Tram 83*
translated by Roland Glasser · DEMOCRATIC REPUBLIC OF CONGO

ILJA LEONARD PFEIJFFER · *La Superba*
translated by Michele Hutchison · NETHERLANDS

RICARDO PIGLIA · *Target in the Night*
translated by Sergio Waisman · ARGENTINA

SERGIO PITOL · *The Art of Flight* · *The Journey* · *The Magician of Vienna* · *Mephisto's Waltz: Selected Short Stories*
translated by George Henson · MEXICO

EDUARDO RABASA · *A Zero-Sum Game*
translated by Christina MacSweeney · MEXICO

ZAHIA RAHMANI · *"Muslim": A Novel*
translated by Matthew Reeck · FRANCE/ALGERIA

C.F. RAMUZ · *Jean-Luc Persecuted*
translated by Olivia Baes · SWITZERLAND

JUAN RULFO · *The Golden Cockerel & Other Writings*
translated by Douglas J. Weatherford · MEXICO

TATIANA RYCKMAN · *The Ancestry of Objects* · USA

JESSICA SCHIEFAUER · *Girls Lost*
translated by Saskia Vogel · SWEDEN

OLEG SENTSOV · *Life Went On Anyway*
translated by Uilleam Blacker · UKRAINE

MIKHAIL SHISHKIN · *Calligraphy Lesson: The Collected Stories*
translated by Marian Schwartz, Leo Shtutin, Mariya Bashkatova, Sylvia Maizell · RUSSIA

ÓFEIGUR SIGURÐSSON · *Öræfi: The Wasteland*
translated by Lytton Smith · ICELAND

MIKE SOTO · *A Grave Is Given Supper: Poems* · USA

MÄRTA TIKKANEN · *The Love Story of the Century*
translated by Stina Katchadourian · SWEDEN

FORTHCOMING FROM DEEP VELLUM

AMANG · *Raised by Wolves*
translated by Steve Bradbury · TAIWAN

MARIO BELLATIN · *Mrs. Murakami's Garden*
translated by Heather Cleary · MEXICO

MAGDA CARNECI · *FEM*
translated by Sean Cotter · ROMANIA

MIRCEA CĂRTĂRESCU · *Solenoid*
translated by Sean Cotter · ROMANIA

MATHILDE CLARK · *Lone Star*
translated by Martin Aitken · DENMARK

LOGEN CURE · *Welcome to Midland: Poems* · USA

PETER DIMOCK · *Daybook from Sheep Meadow* · USA

CLAUDIA ULLOA DONOSO · *Little Bird*, translated by Lily Meyer · PERU/NORWAY

LEYLÂ ERBIL · *A Strange Woman*
translated by Nermin Menemencioğlu · TURKEY

ROSS FARRAR · *Ross Sings Cheree & the Animated Dark: Poems* · USA

FERNANDA GARCIA LAU · *Out of the Cage*
translated by Will Vanderhyden · ARGENTINA

ANNE GARRÉTA · *In/concrete*
translated by Emma Ramadan · FRANCE

GOETHE · *Faust, Part One*
translated by Zsuzsanna Ozsváth and Frederick Turner · GERMANY

PERGENTINO JOSÉ · *Red Ants: Stories*
translated by Tom Bunstead and the author · MEXICO

JUNG YOUNG MOON · *Arriving in a Thick Fog*
translated by Mah Eunji and Jeffrey Karvonen · SOUTH KOREA

TAISIA KITAISKAIA · *The Nightgown & Other Poems* · USA

DMITRY LIPSKEROV · *The Tool and the Butterflies*
translated by Reilly Costigan-Humes & Isaac Stackhouse Wheeler · RUSSIA

FISTON MWANZA MUJILA · *The Villain's Dance*, translated by Roland Glasser · *The River in the Belly: Selected Poems*, translated by Bret Maney · DEMOCRATIC REPUBLIC OF CONGO

GORAN PETROVIĆ · *At the Lucky Hand, aka The Sixty-Nine Drawers*
translated by Peter Agnone · SERBIA

LUDMILLA PETRUSHEVSKAYA · *Kidnapped: A Crime Story*, translated by Marian Schwartz · *The New Adventures of Helen: Magical Tales*, translated by Jane Bugaeva · RUSSIA

JULIE POOLE · *Bright Specimen: Poems from the Texas Herbarium* · USA

MANON STEFAN ROS · *The Blue Book of Nebo* · WALES

ETHAN RUTHERFORD · *Farthest South & Other Stories* · USA

MUSTAFA STITOU · *Two Half Faces*
translated by David Colmer · NETHERLANDS

BOB TRAMMELL · *The Origins of the Avant-Garde in Dallas & Other Stories* · USA